Jack Rubin is a police officer. He is dismissed after five years, accused of accepting bribes. He sets up in business as a private investigator and soon finds that his main occupation is to collect bad debts and harass vulnerable losers. However, his luck seems to turn when he takes on Mohammed Ali Malik, a Pakistani, as his partner.

Rubin, an atheist from a Jewish family, is a totally amoral tough guy and womaniser, and Malik, a Muslim and family man, loyal, frightened of his own shadow, are chalk and cheese. Yet, in spite of deep differences, their partnership seems to succeed. They have agreed one rule: never to discuss religion - and always to make their own tea and coffee.

WHITE MEAT

Jack Rubin

WHITE MEAT

EMMA
STERN
PUBLISHING

An Emma Stern Publication

A CIP catalogue record for this title is available from the British Library.

ISBN: 978-1-911224-05-1

This is a work of fiction. Names, characters, places and incidents originate from
the writer's imagination. Any resemblance to actual persons, living or dead, is
purely coincidental.

Published in 2016

Emma Stern Publishing
107 Fleet Street
London
EC4A 2AB

www.emmastern.com
www.facebook.com/emmasternpublishing
Email: editorial@emmastern.com
Email: marketing@emmastern.com

Printed in Great Britain

Chapter One

'Some people don't seem to have homes to go to.'

The caretaker was hanging about in the corridor, making plenty of noise. He was telling me it was time to get the hell out of the office, he wanted to go home. Well, the pub, anyway, because as soon as the building is clear he strides out along Greene Street to the *Rat and Parrot*.

My colleague, Malik, usually stays late in the office too but today he had gone home early. Reluctantly, because it was a family gathering, and he doesn't enjoy family gatherings, which always seem to end in tears and recriminations.

I nodded at the caretaker as I passed him on the corridor but I did not speak. And he knows better than to try to engage me in small or clever talk about not having a home to go to. He thinks he owns the building, the scruffy bastard, especially when the owner is away on one of his frequent holidays. The owner, Burnham, likes trips to the Maldives or the Seychelles, especially in the cold winter months. And who can blame him? I am not envious of Burnham, or of anyone else for that matter, but there are times when I could do with a winter break myself.

I went down the steps to the large oak front door, and

stepped out into the street. The evening was cold but not unpleasantly so. It was half past eight in the evening and had been dark since about half six. Soon it would be time to go through the ritual of changing the clocks and then the evenings would be lighter.

Today I had parked the car behind the building. This is not my usual place but I'd been out in the afternoon and to save time I'd opted for Ramsden Lane on my return. There were double yellow lines but they were broken and if a warden gave me a ticket I would fight the case in court. I had counted on wardens knocking off early and this proved to be the case today.

My office is one of many in a large Victorian building that had once been a place where merchants priced, sold and then despatched worsted cloth to other parts of the country and to the furtherest shores of Empire. The products were sent initially by rail, from the station across Station Square. The station, the square and the chambers are the one part of the town that was not vandalised and destroyed in the 'sixties and seventies by what were known as property developers.

I turned the corner into Northumberland Street and immediately right again into Ramsden Lane. The car was still there. It isn't much to look at, the motor, and would not do anything for my image if I ever decided to have an image. OK, it's a solid Volvo, and it's mine and I like it.

I unlocked the door. Nothing so sophisticated as central locking. I eased myself into the driving seat and proceeded to remove the lock that covers the hand brake and the gear change lever.

Then the passenger door was opened. I bunched the keys in my fist, ready for action. I need not have bothered. It was a female and on first glance it looked as if she couldn't have knocked the skin off a rice pudding.

'Yes?' I said.

'Hello, big boy,' she said.

I shook my head.

'Not tonight, darling.'

'I give you good time,' she said.

Next thing I know she's on the passenger seat.

I was able to smell her cheap cologne. And she reeked of cigarette smoke too. Not that this puts me off. I am no stranger to *nostalgie de la boue.*

'I think you'd better get out again,' I said.

I looked in the rear view mirrors, suspecting that this could be a set up. I saw no one but, then, I'd not seen the tart when I had opened the Volvo. Experience teaches that in modern towns and cities vigilance is always sensible.

'Not tonight, Josephine,' I said.

'You no like sex?'

'Sure,' I said. 'Very much. But not enough to pay for it.'

'I give what you ask,' she said.

It was then that I noted the careful formal use of English. This bird did not have a full grasp of the language.

9

I reached over her, to open the door, and was assailed by the cigarette smoke and the cheap cologne.

As I leaned over, the tart tried to kiss me on the cheek, missed, and finished up giving me a peck on my ear. In any other circumstance, I'd not have complained; after all the ear, especially the lobe, is an erogenous zone. Come to think of it, most of my body is an erogenous zone.

'Out you go,' I said, pushing the door open.

'No,' she whispered.

'Yes,' I said.

She made no move to get out of the motor. I shoved her, gently at first. That did not work, so I pushed a bit harder. She started to whimper.

'Start crying and I swear I'll beat the shit out of you,' I said.

It was not because she was a tart, hawking her duck for money, that I pretended to be rough with her. The reason was that I felt peckish and wanted to get home and prepare a meal. Sure, I could have eaten out or ordered a takeaway, but sometimes bachelors want to cook something at home, if only to prove they can still manage it.

'I give you for ten bucks,' she said.

I smiled.

'That sounds like good value for money,' I said, 'but like I told you, I don't pay for it. Not directly, anyway.'

We always pay, indirectly; take a bird out on the spree, pay for her food and booze, and that is indirect payment.

'Please, to give me the ten bucks,' the tart said.

Her command of English had not improved in the past few minutes.

She rubbed her nose. That was evidence enough. She wanted money to buy white powder to shove up her nostrils. Lots of prostitutes – so I am led to believe – are drug addicts, which is the way their protectors like it, to keep the poor bitches on a short leash. Did I say protectors? What is wrong with the traditional word – *pimps*?

I reached up and switched on the car's internal light. My intention was to take a tenner from my wallet. With the light on, I could see the girl better. I would not say that I was shocked by what I saw – I am never shocked; surprised, sometimes, but never shocked. Her long hair was black and straight. With my left hand I passed the note, and with my right I pulled at her hair. Which was not hair, but a wig. The real thing underneath was short, blond, cropped like a boy's hair.

'Do you have a name?'I said.

'Sir?'

'What is your name?'

'Anna. Now I go.'

I shook my head slowly.

'You're not going anywhere, Anna. If that is really your name. You stay here, girl.'

'If I will not make plenty money then he will beat me.'

That clinched it. There was a pimp.

I grabbed the girl's wrist and exerted pressure. She let out a squeal.

'How old are you, Anna?'

'Please, I go now.'

'What is your age?' I said, making it easier for her to understand.

'My hand. There is pain.'

'Your neck will have pain very soon. Tell the truth. How old are you, Anna?'

'I have seventeen years,' she said, translating literally.

'Try again,' I said.

'It is true. Seventeen.'

I slapped her across the face. Not too hard, not as if she were a man. But hard enough to let her understand I did not believe her.

'Your age, girl. How old are you?'

She tried to cower but that is not easy when someone is sitting within the confines of a Volvo, being held by the wrists, and likely to be slapped.

'How old are you, Anna?' I said again.

'Fourteen,' she whimpered. 'Fourteen years. Please let me go now, sir, please.'

I did not let her go, but I did release her wrist.

She relaxed a little. I slapped her very hard across her face.

She fell back against the door. I grabbed her by her short, faux-leather coat, and pulled her toward me.

'How old are you?' I said again. It was becoming like some kind of mantra.

There were tears on her cheeks. 'I have fourteen years. It is is the truth. Fourteen.'

Now I had to believe her. It was what I had suspected as soon as I'd yanked off the wig.

'I go now, please.'

I switched on the ignition, looked round carefully to see if anyone had entered Ramsden Lane, or if a man, Anna's pimp, was lurking in a doorway. It was all quiet.

After first turning off the car's internal light, I engaged first gear and pulled away slowly, my eyes peeled for trouble. I turned right, away from the Square and the railway station, and drove by a circuitous route before joining the main road to my place. Yes, I should have made a bee-line for the central police station. That would have been the sensible thing to have done. But I am not always sensible, and I was not assured that Anna would get the assistance she needed if she was dropped there. Probably be coddled by some lesbian sergeant with moustaches.

As soon as I had been certain in my mind that Anna was really only fourteen years old, I had decided to take her home. Don't seek to know the reason why, because even now I do not know what made me act the way I did. I'm no do-gooder, did not want to save the child from a fate worse than death (which in any case it isn't) and I certainly had no wish to have sexual or any other kind of congress. I believe in nothing, but nor am I yet

13

completely an animal.

'Please! Where you take me now?'

I did not answer. I was in fact taking her up to my place on the moors, out of town, to an old farmhouse which I purchased for a song. It is draughty, cold, lacks gas, and you would not be far wrong if you called it a dump. Well, a dump for you maybe but home to me. At my age, hotel rooms no longer hold attraction, unless it's for an assignation with a woman. What is my age? Slap me hard and I would tell you to mind your own business. Ask what kind of women attract me, and I will tell you - those with a pulse. But they have to be over the age of consent, and little Anna, clutching her black wig, stinking still of cigarette smoke and cheap cologne, had most definitely not yet reached the age of consent. Poor little cow.

Chapter Two

'Bring Mona with you,' I said.

'Mona?'

"She's still your wife, isn't she?"

'Yes, but what about the tart?'

I'd explained to Malik that I had, as they say, rescued a young prostitute. I felt like William Ewart Gladstone who used to finish his work in 10 Downing Street, and then roam the streets of London rescuing what the Victorians called 'fallen women'. Let a PM try that today. The media would eat the poor bastard alive.

What I had not yet told Malik was Anna's age. It was early in the morning, and I didn't want him to break out in a lather.

'I need Mona to act as a baby sitter,' I said.

Malik laughed out loud.

'Is she a tart or a baby?' he asked.

'Both,' I said. 'Get up here and I'll explain.'

Within thirty minutes his Merc was pulling on to the unpaved area outside the cottage. I noted that Mona, who used to dress in traditional Muslim or Pakistani garb, had of late taken to skirts and blouses.

Anna was in the bedroom, the spare. I had locked the door on her and secured the windows. For several hours of the night she had screamed and moaned. She needed a fix. Well, she was not going to get it from me. I do not do drugs, and never have. And as for plying children with drugs, no way, Jose. Let me tell you this: anyone who sells or gives drugs of addiction to youngsters, can expect no pity from me. Broken patellas and dislocated shoulders, certainly, but no pity and no licence.

'So where's the tart?' Malik asked cheerfully.

'Malik!' Mona said, quietly and in a disapproving voice.

'In bed. At least, she was when I last looked.'

I unlocked the bedroom door. For a moment I had the feeling Anna might have escaped. But no, she was there, huddled, in the foetal position.

'Time to rise and shine,' I said.

Something my mother used to say to me. These days, she does not say much, my mother. Truth to tell, she no longer remembers who I am. She certainly wouldn't remember I used to be a copper. Mind you, I have difficulty remembering that part of my life myself, although it took up five years better spent elsewhere.

Even now I feel resentment. Who wouldn't? I didn't resign; I was kicked off the force.

For a number of reasons. My big mouth, for a start: I couldn't bring myself to use this new mealy-mouthed language.

For me, a spade is a spade. And a rapist is a piece of shit who deserves to be castrated. But rape is not a fate worse than death. Murder is the worst crime possible, and there is no point in referring to it as a little bit of unpleasant behaviour.

OK! OK! No argument! Let's admit it. Sometimes I acted a bit rough. I knocked some guys around. But only the kind of low-life shit that deserves a bit of knocking about. There are some people, of both sexes, who do not understand appeals to reason. And don't infer that I beat women. That was never my style. I threatened them but never laid a finger on them. OK! OK! I was known to slap them around a bit. After that, they always talked and usually told the truth.

So what was my style? Honesty and good detective skills. I was never bent. Sure, there were times I took short cuts. Who wouldn't? But I never broke the law, never planted evidence, never lied in court proceedings.

I made enemies, and not only in the criminal fraternity of this city. I was always one move ahead of those bastards. There were many – so I am told – who feared me. Because I could not be bought, that's why. And because, when occasion demands it, I can be fast and furious with my fists. (And how is that for slovenly alliteration? Yeah, I had a decent education. It prepared me for quizzes and crossword puzzles, but not for life, and not life in the lower depths.)

It would seem strange, if you knew nothing of human nature, why being honest should make me enemies among members of the force. But that was the way of things. And then there were the local councillors and civil servants. I have been known to ruffle a few feathers in those dovecotes, I admit. Low lifes do not come from one stratum of society. People with power and wealth can be as crooked as the guy who steals lead from the roof of a church.

Anyway, the day arrived when, without warning, I was called in by Silcock. Irish name, but he was born in England. Mind you, he does, I believe, have a penchant for potatoes. But, then, so do I and the nearest I have been to Ireland is the Wallasey Tunnel.

He pointed to a chair. Silcock's older than me by about twenty years. He has risen to the lofty position of Chief Superintendent, and must have licked a few arses on the way, but it didn't show. Before he was translated to a desk job Silcock was a damned good detective. Isn't that the way of things? Find a good detective and move him up to a desk job. Promote an effective teacher to be a Head, or a caring nurse to something far removed from the bedside. Little wonder the country is in the parlous state it is.

'Coffee?'

I shook my head.

'Only drink one cup of coffee a day,' I said. I shrugged my shoulders. 'Well, maybe two cups, if there's a blonde involved.'

'Too much coffee makes you bad-tempered,' Silcock said.

'Not me.' I smiled. 'You know me, Pete. Always sweetness and light.'

He almost smiled. That put me on my guard. This was not just a friendly chat about recent operations.

'Still living in that shitty farmhouse?' he asked.

'It may be shitty to you,' I said, 'but to me it's a palace.'

'You got a mortgage?'

Now I really was on my guard. If Pete Silcock was enquiring after my financial status, there was a reason. I have not been a copper these five years without being sensitive to clues, and that also means verbal clues.

'Should I be calling you Sir?' I asked, except it was not a question.

'Since when did you call anyone Sir? You're even rude to the CC.'

Chief Constable. Sir Radley James Dickerson. Likes to be friendly. Good relations with all ranks. Known in the force as the Big Dick.

Never rude; only plain speaking. My mother, when she had her marbles still, encouraged me never to kowtow. Said I was as good as the next man. At this moment the next man was Chief Superintendent Pete Silcock. He had in his career solved two particularly gruesome murders. The bastards should have been topped, but we live in enlightened times, and that means wearing kid gloves even with killers of the nastiest kind. Both men – would you believe it? - are currently out on parole, and as likely to kill again as they are to take a leak after several pints of beer.

Silcock sighed deeply. The corners of his mouth were turned down. He did not look like a happy bunny. In fact, he didn't look like a bunny at all. He looked like a middle-aged man who spent too much time at his desk, and was fast running to seed.

'Spit it out, Pete,' I said.

'Do you think I enjoy this?' he said.

'It depends on what *this* is.'

He drew in breath.

'You're in deep shit,' he said.

'So what's new?'

'This is no time for joking?'

'Who the hell is joking?'

'You take risks,' Silcock said.

So which detective does not take risks? It goes with the territory, Mr Kent, as the young photographer said to Superman. Considering the San Andreas fault was splitting wide open at the time, that indicated a remarkable degree of aplomb on the young man's part, or downright stupidity. I vote for the latter.

'I get results, Pete.'

'You'd do even better if you stuck to the rules and curbed your tongue.'

I shook my head sadly. He'd get round to the subject in hand soon enough.

'You know me, Pierre. I can't lick arse. There are enough brown noses in this county.'

We are a county force, what used to be known as a constabulary.

'Are you having money problems?' he asked.

'Who doesn't?'

'I want to know,' he answered sternly.

'My bank details are private,' I said. 'Or have you bastards been hacking into my personal details?'

'We are not bastards,' Silcock said, still stern, 'and we did it for a reason.'

That made me sit straight up. Now I was paying his words full attention. I recognise a past tense when I hear one. *We did it for a reason.*

'What the hell's going on?' I asked. 'You guys have been pushing your bloody noses into my........shit!'

'It was necessary.'

'Sure it was,' I sneered.

'Why? Have you anything to hide?'

'That's no answer,' I said.

'This conversation is not being recorded,' Silcock said, assuming his official voice, 'but I must ask you to desist from uttering foul language in the presence of a superior officer.'

Cop talk! I have always tried to avoid it, and have succeeded.

I looked Silcock straight in the eye and he was the first to blink.

'Get it off your chest,' I said.

I was certain he was no longer Pete. No longer even Mr Silcock. This was, I guessed, going to be a reprimand. I was wrong on that score.

Silcock cleared his throat.

'Mr Rubin. I have to officially inform you that you are with immediate effect on suspension from the Police Service of this county. You will with immediate effect hand over to me your documents and all other items belonging to the service.'

'There was a split infinitive in there but I did not consider this the best time to remind him, and, in any case, I hang looser on split infinitives than I used to.

'And what, Chief Superintendent Silcock, if I may make so bold, is the nature of the charge? What is the reason for -'

'Accepting a bribe,' Silcock interrupted.

I burst out laughing

'Me? Take a bribe? You cannot, as the man said, be serious.'

'I'm very serious, Inspector Rubin.'

No more David. No more palsy-walsy.

'It's no go the Yogi-Man, it's no go Blavatsky / All we want is a bank balance and a bit of skirt in a taxi.'

'What are you talking about, you mad bastard?' Silcock said.

I shook my head in mock disgust.

'Chief Superintendent Silcock. I must ask you to desist from uttering foul language in the presence of an inferior officer.'

'As it happens, this is about your bank balance,' he said.

'I hope you went through the proper channels in order to gain access,' I said. 'If you'd asked me, I could have saved you time. I now do internet banking, chip and pin.'

'How much do you have in your personal account?' Silcock asked.

'My personal account? Why, is there another?'

'You tell me,' Silcock said.

'When I last checked, it was about sixty bucks. I'm usually waiting for pay day.'

Silcock opened a drawer and took out a sheet of paper. You didn't need special powers to know it was my bank statement.

I smiled. I was on strong ground.

Silcock handed the sheet over to me. I was still smiling when I looked at the balance. And had the smile wiped immediately.

My balance was sixty grand and sixty bucks. The sixty I knew about. So where in hell's name had the sixty grand come from?

'It's a bank error,' I said. 'I'll soon put it right. These things happen.'

Silcock shook his head, and I'll swear there was sadness in his eyes.

'After five or so good years, and you take a bribe.'

'I have not taken a bribe and you know it,' I said.

'All I know about is the evidence,' Silcock said.

'OK, let's hear it,' I said.

'We have a sworn statement from a bank clerk, to the effect you deposited sixty thousand pounds into your personal account.'

I do not like the term, but I have to admit that I was....yes, gobsmacked!

'She accepted the money and has your signature on a slip.'

I did not speak. Speech is silver but silence is golden. You have the right to remain silent, but......

'You live in a big house. You run a good car. You like skirt.'

'Skirt?'

'Everybody knows you're a ladies man.'

'Would they be happier if I were an uphill gardener?'

'You don't smoke or take alcohol in excess. So where does your salary go?'

'Apart from prostitutes and cocaine?' I said.

'This is no time for levity, Jack'

'Inspector Rubin, if you don't mind,' I said severely, and I was not trying to be funny.

'People talk, Jack,' Silcock said.

Jack! Perhaps I was not as deep in the shit as I had thought.

But I was, almost over my head in liquid faces, and the murmuring I could hear was, 'Don't make waves, don't make waves.'

'Let people talk,' I said. 'I know the truth.'

'People want to know just how you can afford that motor -'

'It's only a top-of-the range BMW,' I told him.

'Series 3, tourer. Asking price £27,000.'

'So I'm frugal. Never take sugar in my tea.'

'And those two weeks in Mauritius.'

'It's too far to travel for just one week,' I said.

I was sailing again. I knew damn well I had never accepted a bribe, though I had been offered them, and could soon clear up this misunderstanding.

'I can't afford Mauritius,' Silcock said, 'not even on my pay.'

'Didn't I mention I don't take milk in my tea, either, and never buy butter or margarine for my bread.'

He flexed his fingers, both hands, as if he were feeling pain in his joints and this was the way to relieve the discomfort.

'So what are we going to do?' he asked, more to himself than to me.

'You can rely on me,' I said. 'I'll do my bit.'

'What do you mean?'

'I'll make some investigations. Get to the bottom of this.'

He shouted angrily: 'You'll do no such thing!'

I was taken aback. Silcock is a man who doesn't usually need to raise his voice. He knows there's more menace in a soft voice, the kind Brando used in *The Godfather*. Make him an

25

offer he can't refuse.

'You are under suspension,' he continued, though not shouting so loudly now. 'This is not your case.'

'It is very much my case,' I insisted hotly. 'Somebody is out to destroy me.'

I knew before Silcock said it what was coming next.

'You're doing a pretty good job of it yourself.' He paused. 'What made you do it, Jack?'

'You're not listening,' I said. 'I have not taken a bribe. Not even a single penny. I've charged people who tried to offer me money. Somebody out there – this bank clerk, or whatever they call them these days – has been paid or threatened to tell lies about me.'

'She's sworn on oath.'

'She's still a liar. What's the bitch's name?'

'You keep away from witnesses,' Silcock said. 'Or I swear I'll nick you myself.'

'I'm going to find out,' I said, anger welling up inside of me.

I don't like to lose control of my emotions. In my line of work it pays to be as objective as possible. But this was something that affected me deeply, and a bank employee was lying, either for a kickback, or from fear. Crooks can place pressure on people. Members of juries are threatened, so why not a humble bank clerk?

'I am going to take this case,' Silcock said. 'If you are telling the truth -'

'I am,' I interrupted.

'If you are telling the truth,' he continued calmly, 'I'll find out who the buggers are who are trying to frame you, and why they are doing that.'

'I'll look at the cases and see who it might be,' I said.

'You'll do nothing of the sort. Hear that, Jack. Nothing of the sort. Take a holiday.'

'I'll use the sixty grand to go to Mauritius,' I grinned.

'Not without your passport, you won't.'

'You mean...?'

'Yes,' Silcock said. 'It's that serious.'

'I'm suspended. You are taking my cards and my passport. I'm not allowed to make investigations. Why don't you chop off my legs?'

'If that becomes necessary,' Silcock said.

'Not funny, mister.'

'Go home,' he said. 'If you intend to travel, let me know. You like islands, don't you?'

In the last year I have visited Mauritius, and, nearer home, Mull, Iona and Lindisfarne. I've also been to the Isle of Dogs, but that doesn't really count. Yes, I like islands. But how did Silcock know? I do not vouchsafe my holiday or weekend plans to him or anyone else. On my off days I fill up the tourer and head north. The guy really had been doing some serious digging.

'Work in the garden,' Silcock said. 'Read those books that

line your shelves.'

Another clue. And one I could have done without learning. Silcock has never been to my place, and I have not talked about my domestic arrangements, so that meant he, or more likely one of his minions, had searched the farmhouse. One of my colleagues, probably, and they had never breathed a single word to me.

'What about my pay?'I asked. 'Or can I spend the sixty big ones?'

'Half pay,' Silcock said. 'Into a savings account we have opened for you.'

'Gee, thanks, boss,'I said in an execrable American accent that owed nothing to the United States.

'Sit at home. Relax in front of the telly.'

'There's just one problem there,' I said. 'I don't have a TV. Or didn't you notice?'

'Christ, they said you were eccentric.'

'Is it eccentric to refuse to fill my brain with shit?'

'In our house it's never off,' he said.

'Moving wallpaper,' I told him. 'And don't blame your children.'

We sat in silence for a short while but two people together in an office cannot maintain silence for long. In any case, I still had a few questions to ask.'

'Will this get into the newspapers?'

'I'll try and keep it quiet,' Silcock said. 'But I guarantee nothing. If you hear your name mentioned on the Six O'clock News, it won't have come from me.'

'Keep it under wraps until I have had time to ask a few questions.'

Silcock stood up suddenly. He banged hard on his desk, upset a cup filled with ball point pens and colour markers.

'Christ, you still don't understand, do you? This is not your case and it never will be. You are suspended. I had to fight to get you to remain on half pay. This is a serious matter. Orders came from above.'

'How high above, Pete?'

'The Big Dick himself.'

Silcock flopped down in his comfortable chair once again.

'Do as I have told you, or you'll go inside. And you don't want that, do you?'

'A handsome chap like me? Young and attractive. With all those hairy sex-starved cons? No way, Pedro.'

'Shouldn't that be Jose?'he asked, looking tired.

'It was a kind of.....joke. You know. '

'No I don't know. But I do know this, Jack. If you are found guilty – and you have not been charged yet, remember – if you are charged and found guilty, you'll go down for some time. Judges may be getting more lenient with real criminals, but they like to punish rotten apples.'

'My job, Pete. My reputation. My career. I must save these.'

'No, Silcock said. 'Saving you is my job. His face was serious. He leaned across the desk. 'I think, Jack, and I say this in all seriousness, that I am your best hope. In fact, I suspect that I am your only hope.'

A small voice in my head told me not to respond. That same voice also told me that the best hope for saving my job, my career, my reputation, was me. Jackis, Jack, Rubin. Inspector in the county police service, now suspended on half pay, my bank account frozen. Yes, I, not Pete Silcock, was my best hope. Somebody was trying to finish me off, and had suborned people to tell lies. I was going to find out who that person or persons was or were – you can accuse me of theft, but you cannot accuse me of weak noun-verb congruence – and I was going to stamp on their bollocks. As the man said: stamp hard enough on their balls, and their hearts and minds will follow after.

But that is another story. Within a couple months Silcock had taken early retirement, with reluctance I was told, and I was out on my ear. No charges, no court appearances – and no job. So what was I to do? I had no trade, no skills. Yes, I became a private detective. A private investigator. P. I. You know, I have never known what title to take. I no longer had a steady monthly salary, and most jobs I obtained were collection of debts. Right now, I still had the mortgage, Malik as a partner, little prospect of earning money, and an under-age tart sleeping in my spare bed.

Welcome, folks, to harsh reality.

Welcome.

Chapter Three

I keep irregular hours, and so I have to take my sleep whenever and wherever I can. I have become accustomed to stealing an hour here and a couple of hours there. And not always, I have to admit, in my own bedroom.

Falling asleep is no problem. I manage to switch off my mind from the problems that face me. This I have to do in my work as a detective. If I didn't know how to switch off, I'd be taking my work home every day, and would become obsessed by it to the exclusion of leisure. I have never wanted murder, blood, knives and guns to invade the privacy of my house and my thoughts.

Although I am boasting at the way I can fall asleep and leave my problems behind, that is not completely true; in fact; one's thoughts follow into dreams. When I awoke two hours later it was from a riotous and crazy dream in which I was on a bus, and the bus was being pursued by screaming police vehicles. What made my situation worse, was that I was completely naked, and none of the other passengers would assist me in any way.

If you think that on waking I tried to analyse my dream, you would be wrong. I don't follow that Freudian stuff. It is a dead end, unscientific. Sometimes, a cigar is just a cigar.

I parked up in a side street. It's a habit of mine. On a single yellow line. But it was evening and little chance of getting a ticket. Malik had wanted to come with me but I convinced him there might be fisticuffs, and he fears physical violence. He's a portly kind of guy and not built for fighting. Not built for running away either, although he does that quite well. I don't like violence all that much but I don't fear it.

I walked round the corner and saw the club.

Flashing neon sign. Lots of light near the entrance.

Welcome, sucker! Come in. Have a drink. Lose your money.

There was a bouncer on the door. A stockily-built black guy. The bouncer had a shaven head, and looked tough.

'You a member, mate?'

'No. I want to be signed in.'

'No problem, mate.'

'That's twice.'

'What?'

'Twice you've referred to me as your mate.'

'So? You got an issue with that?' In the bouncer's eyes was a look of genuine incomprehension.

'Are you going to let me pass?'

The bouncer shrugged his broad shoulders. 'You got a name?'

'Rubin.'

"First name?'

'Mister,' I said.

'Wha'ever,' the bouncer said, and stepped to one side.

He wasn't going to argue with me. Six feet tall, fourteen stones, and muscle where it mattered.

I went into the club. There was a foyer, where a woman offered to take my coat. For a price.

'How much?'

'Fourteen quid,' she said.

"Daylight robbery,' I said, taking off my long black overcoat and handing over a twenty note. 'Keep the change.

Beyond was a bar, and further in, to the back of the club, the casino. Where the real daylight robbery was taking place. Except it was evening, and dark outside.

I went to the bar. Ordered a brandy and ginger ale.

The waiter brought the brandy in a glass and the ginger ale in a small bottle. There was ice in the brandy.

'No ice,' I said, pushing the glass away.

'No ice?'

'Only chavs take ice with brandy,' Rubin said.

'Lots of people take ice,' the waiter said.

'Not me, so take it away.'

The barman wasn't happy but he did as ordered.

After I had poured a little of the ginger ale into the brandy, I turned to survey the bar area. Over the far side there seemed to be some trouble brewing. A young man was shouting the odds and a girl – half naked, as it seemed to me – was cowering against the wall. Yet managing to show defiance, too. There was threat in every contour of the man's body.

I turned and took a sip of the brandy and ginger ale. I heard a slap. Palm against face. I turned again. The girl was holding her cheek bone. The man had not finished. He moved forward to strike the girl again.

'Don't do that, mister,' I said, my voice loud enough to quieten the room.

The young man turned to find out who was giving him orders.

He did not have to look far; I advanced on him with steady and determined step.

'Why can't I learn to mind my own business?

'Who the fuck are -'

The young guy never completed his sentence. I struck him a heavy blow in the solar plexus, where it really hurts. He bent double, his jaw undefended. I know a good target when I see one. A swift movement of my right arm and fist struck jawbone. There was an audible crack. The guy went over backwards and his head struck the corner of a table. He lay there moaning.

I looked at the girl.

'Mebbe you had better go home,' I said.

The girl nodded. Without a word of thanks she ran out of the bar and into the street.

A couple of bouncers, both white, both with shaven heads – did these guys think a shaven head automatically endowed them with toughness - closed in on me.

I held up my arms.

'I've no argument with you guys,' I said.

'The two bouncers did not approach too near. They had seen what I had done to the pillock on the floor, moaning with pain, blood issuing from a cut on his forehead.

'The Boss wants a word,' one bouncer, the taller of the two, said.

'And I want a word with your boss,' I said.

I could tell there was not going to be a fight with these two.

'He wants a word,' a bouncer said, as if that were enough to command me.

'Shouldn't you be moving this twat outside?' I said.

'Fuck him!' a bouncer said.

'Not while there are dogs on the street,' I said.

There was a ripple of amusement from the people sitting in the bar.

'Let's go,' the smaller of the two men urged. Clearly he took the word of the Boss as something to be instantly obeyed.

'OK,' I said. 'Take me to your Leader.'

The bouncers led me up some stairs. There were old black and white photographs of actors who had played gangsters in movies of the thirties and forties. Bogart. George Raft. James Cagney. Edward G. Robinson. Mike Mazurki. John Garfield.

The taller of the two guys stopped at a door, knocked quietly and respectfully, and waited.

'Come in.'

The room had two-way mirrors on a couple of sides. The guy at the desk, smoking a cigar, could see clearly into the bar area on one side and the casino on the other.

'You asked us to bring him up, Mr Sutcliffe.'

'Give you trouble, did he?' Sutcliffe asked, an amused smile playing on his lips.

'No, Sir.'

'Came as quiet as a lamb,' the other bouncer said.

'He surely doesn't look like a lamb,' Sutcliffe said.

He bJack out cigar smoke. One of the bouncers started to cough.

Without waiting to be asked, I sat down on a chair at the desk, directly opposite Sutcliffe.

'Blow smoke in my direction,' I said.

The bouncers looked concerned. Nobody stood tall against Mr Sutcliffe. But to their surprise, Sutcliffe burst out laughing.

'I liked the way you dealt with the guy in the bar,' he said.

'He slapped that kid.'

'Things like that worry you, do they?' Sutcliffe asked.

I said nothing.

'I cold use a guy like you,' Sutcliffe said.

'You sound like the heavy in a B movie,' I said.

Sutcliffe smiled.

'OK, you guys,' he said to the bouncers. 'You can resume your duties,'

As soon as the two men had left, both Sutcliffe and I stood up. We shook hands.

'Well, Jack. After all this time.'

'I see you're still in the gambling business, Humphrey,' I said, turning to look out of the window overlooking the casino.

'Harry. It's Harry now,' Sutcliffe said.

'What's wrong with Humphrey?'

'As a name, nothing. I like it. But these days, people think it sounds a bit....you know, poncy.'

'Tell that to Bogart,' I said.

'Fashions change, Jack,' he said.

'You haven't joined the other side, have you?' I said.

'No way!' Sutcliffe said. 'But Harry seems to sound better. At least, it attracts no comments.'

I surveyed the room.

'So how's business, Humph?'

'It's not easy,' Sutcliffe answered. 'I'm not big enough.'

'What do you need to be bigger?' I asked.

'An injection of cash,' Sutcliffe said, seriously, 'and you as my general manager.' When I did not answer, Sutcliffe asked: 'Interested?'

'What's it pay, Humph?'

'Sure you won't have a cigar?' Sutcliffe said.

I shook my head. 'This is an office, a place of work, and smoking is forbidden by law.'

'To hell with that!' Sutcliffe said. 'It's also a place where I sometimes sleep.'

'With?'

'Whichever one of the paid help is willing,' Sutcliffe said, and he smiled expansively. 'So what do you say, Jack? Eh?'

'I say this,' I replied. 'I could kill a drink.'

'Brandy? That still your tipple.'

He knew damn well it was; he had observed me as soon as I'd entered the bar.

Sutcliffe spoke into a walkie-talkie.

'Trace! A bottle of brandy. Cognac. Ginger ale, Canada Dry, six bottles.' He paused. 'I'll have a pot of tea. My usual. And.....no ice with the brandy.'

Sutcliffe snapped off the walkie-talkie.

'Tea?' I said.

'No choice, Jack. Gut rot. I have to keep well away from the hard stuff. Even beer sets me off.'

A girl dressed in a short black skirt and a thin white blouse came in, carrying a tray. She was wearing what looked suspiciously like a school tie.

Humphrey had always displayed a taste for jail bait.

That was why I had come to see him.

Chapter Four

'Right, girl!' I said. 'Out of that bed.'

Anna groaned. Unlike me, she was no early riser.

'It's a beautiful day. The sun is shining.'

'I not liking the sun shining,' she said, screwing up her eyes and diving back beneath the duvet.

'Five minutes,' I said.

I went into the kitchen. The porridge was in a pan on the stove. It had been steeping in cold water all night. Now the water had been absorbed. There was enough for two people.

I could hear the shower running. The child, for Anna was still a child, had surfaced. I went to the door, to make sure she really was in the shower, and not pretending. I need not have bothered. Anna took personal hygiene seriously.

She came into the kitchen.

'What that smell, Mr Rubin?'

'Kippers,' I said. 'Sit down.'

Anna was dressed in a plain white tee shirt and very short denim shorts, ragged at the edges, as if she had cut them down, but I knew one could buy them like that, ready made and ready ragged. Just as there are jeans with holes. I don't claim to understand fashion. Have never worn denim in any form.

But I understand a little about the law. Chances were, I was not only harbouring a child well below the age of consent, but also, in all likelihood, an illegal immigrant, a trafficked person.

I had deliberately abstained from asking Anna about here home and her background. Better to get her back on her feet first. I noticed that she had, in just a few days, put on weight. She was still slim but she had a fuller face, and looked more like a child now, and less the mangy tart who had first propositioned me in Ramsden Lane.

Anna piled sugar on to her porridge. Could have been worse – could have been maple syrup. I take my porridge straight, nothing added save a pinch of salt.

Now the kippers were ready. The smell pervaded the farm house. The smell of food I don't mind. Not even when the food is kippers. These had been filleted.

She watched me put butter on the fish, and a liberal dash of pepper, and proceeded to do the same. After an initial sniff, she discovered that she too liked kippers for breakfast, and soon wolfed the lot.

'Where is your home?'I said, keeping my voice low and gentle.

'Lithuania,' she said. 'Vilnius.'

'Are you....you just couldn't be Jewish, could you?'

She looked puzzled.

41

'Are you Jewish, Anna?'

A look of hatred appeared on her young face and she spat.

'Jew people,' she said.

I smiled tolerantly.

'My mother is from Lithuania. She is Jewish.'

Her eyes opened wide.

'You are Lithuanian Jew?'

'My mother, not me. She is a Litvak.'

'Where is mother now?'

'She is....sick. In hospital.'

That was all she needed to know.

Anna had no reason to know that my mother was in a home for old people suffering from severe dementia. She was in a place in one of the valleys of the Lake District, unable to enjoy the wonderful scenery outside the thick windows and the locked doors. Unable even to remember her son, when I visited her. The last time, she had introduced a male care worker as her son Jack.

I stood up and clapped my hands.

'OK, girl. Clean your teeth. Get your coat.'

'Where we go, Mr Rubin?'

'Malik's place.'

She smiled. 'I like Mona. She make good food.'

On the drive into town I kept thinking what my next move

might be. I could not take Anna all the way back to Lithuania. Nor could I drop her off somewhere and leave her to fend for herself.

I needed to know more about her.

Half way to town I pulled in to a lay-by.

Anna looked at me with a surprised look on her face.

'You like sex. Mr Rubin?'

The poor little bitch. In her brief experience, stopping in a lay-by meant having some form of sex.

While I wasn't lost for words – I'm never that – I was unsure of how best to proceed. After all, this was my first experience of rescuing a child prostitute. Watching de Niro in *Taxi Driver* had not prepared me for this. Nor my few years as a cop. This hot potato would have been passed to a female officer, a child psychologist, and some form of care worker, and they would, between them, have made a hash of it. I had to admit to myself that my chances of success were equally slim, but at least I'd try not to disturb the child more than she was already. And if I could keep her away from the white powder long enough for her not to crave it, that would be a small victory.

This was going to be a long interview, sitting there in the Volvo while commuters raced by as if there were a prize to win by seeing who could drive fastest into town. I had a plan of action laid out in my mind: soft questions to start with; move on to the tougher stuff; and finally discover who her pimp was and where he lived, or at least where he had kept Anna a prisoner. Once I had data on the pimp, I would know exactly what to do. And what I planned would not involve the police service, as we

43

must now learn to call the constabulary. What I planned involved at least one ruptured spleen, several fractured bones, and the contents of a scrotum that would not be of any use for several years, if ever again.

Chapter Five

'Perhaps Ives can help us,' I said.

'Why should Ives help us?' Malik asked sulkily.

'Yes, I know he's in the business, but as far as I know he doesn't run children.'

'How do you know?' Malik said. 'We don't know much about Ives.'

That was true. Ives often crosses our paths, but only briefly, and when he wants something.

Ives is six foot plus of black Caribbean hard man. He has fists like shovels and you can see by looking at them that he uses them often. According to the police, who keep tabs on Ives – OK, they harass him – Ives controls drugs and prostitutes in two major cities, and has connections in London as well.

That's as may be. It is no business of mine. In my experience, Ives makes a lot of money threatening to take people to court for compensation. Here's how it works. He purchases an item on credit, but does not keep up the payments. When he is threatened with court action, he writes a letter threatening to seek compensation on the grounds of poor service and racial discrimination. Except he does not write the letters. I do, on his behalf. I went to school and learned to write; Ives was taken out of school at fourteen and incarcerated in a special institution for naughty boys, and he still carries the grievance. A couple of letters and the other party always caves in.

'I think we should keep guys like Ives,' Malik said.

'You've never liked him, have you?' I said.

'What's to like?' Malik asked. 'He's a gangster.'

I knew what Malik meant. Ives was a dangerous man. His business were far from legit. Yet in his contempt for authority, and the sheer chutzpah of his ways of working, his audacity and insolence, well, I admit to liking him. Not entirely. I'm no sentimental fool, but you have to give credit to a young man who refuses to bow the head or knuckle under, no matter what. He once told me stories of what went on in that young offenders; institution, how the screws not only beat him, but tortured him, and still he refused to bend the knee.

Now, at the age of twenty-seven, Ives is a very rich man, and could be even richer if he learned to play the system and get in with the crooks who run legit businesses. But that kind of accommodation Ives calls selling out.

'You know, Malik. I think Ives will die in prison.,' I said.

'So when do we go round and see him?'

Malik could tell I had made up my mind.

I picked up the telephone and called a number in Norman Road. A woman answered.

'I want to talk to Delroy,' I said.

'Who you want?'

'Delroy, your nephew. Or Mr Ives, or whatever his name is this week.' And added: 'Don't you worry, I'm not the police.'

'I don't know where that bwaay is,' she said.

I gave her my name and told her to contact her nephew.

'OK, Mr Rubin, I do that. But I aint his auntie. I'm his niece.'

There are cases where an aunt is younger than a niece. Depends on how sexually active a family is.

'What is your plan, Mr Rubin?'Malik asked.

We maintain quite a high level of formality, my business partner and I.

'You know my methods, Watson,' I said.

He didn't ask me to explain the allusion and I did not volunteer.

My methods are what I learned as a cop. Amass as much information as possible. Some of it - most of it – would prove to have no value, but among the shale and muck there might be a bright shining light, and it might just be a diamond. But I always add something else to the mix. I stir up trouble. I want people to know I'm about. In many instances, they come to me. Or they did when I was a detective with the force. Now that I'm in private business, I get very few visitors, few cases. Jack Rubin Associates needs a paying case, and pretty soon, and here I was, working, as they say in legal services, pro bono. For nothing. And for a little kid from Lithuania.

47

Sure, a child from Lithuania. But more than that. Trafficked. Made false promises. Brought over here ostensibly for a short holiday, and then put on drugs and made to work. And the first two occasions she had tried to refuse, she had had shit knocked out of her. It could have been a daughter of mine, if I had a daughter.

The telephone rang.

Malik skipped across the room in a way that belied his port;y figure.

Jack Rubin Associates. Mr Stern speaking. How may I help you?'

I could just make out Ives telling Malik to put the Boss on.

Malik doesn't like it when someone suggests he works for me. We are partners. Nevertheless, he passed the handset over to me. I sat down.

'Ives.'

'Mr Rubin. You called me.'

'I need information, Ives. I have a girl. Fourteen years old. She's been working as a prostitute.'

'Where?' Ives asked.

'Here. She tried to pick me up the other evening,' I said.

'And?' he said, with a loud guffaw.

'And nothing. She's fourteen years old.'

'Her age worry you, Mr Rubin?'

'Nothing worries me, Ives. I'm not a copper, not a moralist.

48

But there are one or two things at which

I draw the line.'

'Me too,' Ives said.

'There was no point if he had children in his stable. The one time I had tried to broach the subject, Ives had hotly denied he was involved in running tarts and distributing drugs.

'Who do you know who runs children,' I said.

'Where you are, I have no dealings at all.'

I knew that Nottingham was his main base. That was probably where he was calling from.

'Yes, but can you give me as lead? I need your help, Ives.'

'The town is run by guys from the east,' he said.

'East? Eastern Europe? The Near East?The Middle East? East Anglia.'

'Kurds and Iraqis. But there's also a gang of Russians.'

'What do you mean, Russians?'

'East Europe. They got the right to reside here. Work here. Poles. Romas.'

'Tell me, Ives, in confidence, give me a name. Not some guy who runs children, but knows a guy who does.'

I heard him exhale breath heavily. He was thinking.

When Ives spoke again, his voice was softer.

'Naseem Khan. Savile Town.'

'He would know?'

Yeah! Try him at the Pioneer Garage.'

'I'll do that,' I said. 'Thanks, Ives. I owe you one.'

'You owe me nothing, Mr Rubin, nothing at all. Jus' glad to oblige a friend.'

'I'll not argue,' I said.

'One thing,' Ives said. 'Who was the guy answered your phone?'

'That was Malik,' I said.

'That aint the name he gave.'

'Sometimes he calls himself Mr Stern.'

Chapter Six

It was like going to a foreign country.

There were no white faces in Savile Town. None to be seen on the streets,anyway. The shops all had signs in Urdu or Punjabi, and sometimes both. I soon lost count of the takeaways, selling pizzas, shish kebabs and lamb curries. No pork butchers in Savile Town. And I, despite my upbringing, and fond of bacon, ham and just about any product from the versatile pig. As far as I'm concerned, dietary laws are for nomads wandering forty years in the desert. Forty years, just to get across Sinai. I ask you. An IDS tank achieves it in a few hours.

Pioneer Garage had a large forecourt, but there was hardly a space to put another vehicle. Naseem Khan appeared to be doing good business. Of course, appearances are not the whole story. There was a lot of activity, men of all ages walking about, or working on motor cars and vans. There was shouting and laughter, but nothing I could understand; it was all in Punjabi.

I had suggested to Malik that he come alone to talk to Naseem Khan. He had shaken his head vigorously. It's his main source of physical exercise.

'But he'll open up to you,' I said.

'No way,'Malik assured me. 'You don't understand these people. Especially the older generation. Those who remember the Raj or heard about it from their parents.'

I think I understood more than Malik intimated. I'd seen it in Africa, the way the Indians, as they are always called there, sucked up to the whites and held down fast on the blacks. That will have changed, now that South Africa has majority rule, but I'll wager the general rule still applies.

As if by a miracle, Malik found a space to park his battered Mercedes Benz. We walked to the large roll door and saw a sign saying 'Office', the only English word for miles around. A tall man stepped between us and the door. he was not wearing overalls; there was no oil on those large hands. the guy was a bouncer. What kind of garage proprietor is it that needs muscle to protect him?

Words were exchanged in Punjabi and finally, without smiling or offering a word of greeting, the hard man showed us through to an inner office. It was not so much an office, more a comfortable lounge. It was dark and curtained, and as we were ushered inside I saw a bearded man rise from a couch. He had clearly been sleeping.

Muscles opened a curtain. Then, without a word, he went out. The bearded old man signalled for us to sit down. Malik and he shook hands. Malik spoke in Punjabi and I heard my name. Now it was my turn to shake hands. The bearded one was introduced as Naseem Khan.

Naseem and Malik spoke together. I could not understand a single word. I knew then that my coming was a waste of time.

The younger man returned with a large metal tray, on which was a jug of water and three glasses. He poured out water. I noted that he gave water first to me, then to Naseem and finally to Malik.

'So, Mr Rubin,' Naseem said. 'You are a police officer.'

I caught sight of Malik's twitching face.

'Yes,' I said, and did not elaborate on the lie.

By now I understand my business partner. He likes to elaborate. A third-class honours degree from a provincial university soon becomes a a Master's from Oxford, and a two-week holiday in Syria a couple of years conducting business successfully in Damascus, with regular visits to Beirut, often through withering gunfire. In short, Malik is a liar, usually in the interests of Jack Rubin Associates, and always in the interests of Mohammed Ali Malik.

'I can assure you, Mr Khan,' I said that anything that passes between us today is strictly confidential.

Malik started to interpret but Naseem held up a hand imperiously.

'I have your word on that, Mr Rubin?'

'Beyond a peradventure, Mr Khan,' I said, knowing Naseem would not understand, and Malik would not be able to translate.

The guy smiled and I smiled back, and neither one of us was fooled.

'I have no objection,' I said, 'if you and my colleague wish to continue speaking in Punjabi.'

'I prefer Urdu,' Naseem said. 'It is more....what is the word?'

'Nuanced,' I said. 'Better able to express deep, subtle things, such as concepts, ideas.'

I'm no different from Malik when it comes to laying on the lard, though in this instance lard is not the best choice of word.

'Yes, Mr Rubin, you are right, of course.'

He sounded like Alec Guinness playing Sherif Hussein the desert movie. Hussein was a subtle guy, too, and finished up on the throne of Iraq, and Alec Guinness had more secrets in his private life than is good for one man to carry.

For the next twenty minutes the two men carried on an earnest discussion, with the occasional nod to me when a sentence or phrase in English was used.

Finally, Naseem clapped his hands together and stood up

quickly in a fashion that belied his years. I'd put him down at about sixty-five years, but the grey beard may have made him seem older.. Malik also stood up but with considerably less agility. That boy needs to lose several pounds. I doubt that he will ever succeed, not as long as there are pizza and kebab outlets on the streets, and certainly not while he is married to Mona, who feeds him in a fashion you'd swear was learned in the fattening houses of Nigeria.

'It was good of you to come, Superintendent Rubin,' Naseem said. 'If you ever wish to purchase a motor vehicle -'

'I shall not hesitate to come here, Mr Khan.'

'You are – if I may say so,' Khan said quietly, 'rather young to have risen to the rank of -'

Again I interrupted.

'I was on a graduate recruitment scheme,' I said. 'Fast track.'

'Ah yes! And which university was that, Mr Rubin?'

'Oxford,' I said, without hesitation, without blushing, and without shame.

I have learned what it is impresses these guys.

After several handshakes we finally found ourselves back in the Merc. Malik was surprised and pleased. During our stay the car had been washed outside and vacced on the inside.

As soon as we were out of Savile Town I ordered Malik to pull over. I wanted to know what he had learned. There had to be something good from more than twenty minutes.

His cell phone rang. Malik looked at the print out.

Mona,' he said.

She who must be obeyed.

Their conversation was in Punjabi. I understood not a word but I could detect agitation in Malik's voice.

He slapped the phone back into its slide.

'What's wrong?' I said.

Malik sighed and wiped his brow with as large handkerchief.

'The kid.'

'Anna?'

'Yes.'

'Yes, what?'

I was getting agitated too.

'Has she run away? Has she....escaped?'

'Two guys....came to the house,' Malik said. 'Grabbed her and took her away?'

'What kind of guys, Malik?' I said quietly. 'Pakistanis?'

'Two white guys. They threatened Mona and snatched Anna.'

'Let's get back,' I said. 'Get this lump of metal into gear.'

'It's automatic transmission,' Malik said.

He looked as sad as I felt. But I also felt deep anger.

'The bastards,' I said.

It was time for me to talk to Mr Silcock. He did not go to Oxford, or any university but he is a police Superintendent. A proper one.

Chapter Seven

'I'll come round to your place.'

Silcock was whispering into his telephone.

That surprised me. That he should want to visit me at home and that he should whisper. He is famous in the police force as a man with a loud voice.

Silcock came in an unmarked car and alone. I saw him arrive but let him to come to the door and knock.

'Beer?' I said.

He declined with a shake of his head.

'The quack warned me off. And cigarettes. Told me I'd be dead within months if I didn't get my blood pressure down.'

'And?'

I've quit alcohol but there isn't a day goes by I couldn't kill a ciggie.'

I went to the kitchen and came back with two glasses of cold water.

'What's that humming noise?' He cocked an ear. 'Can you hear it?'

'It's the generator,' I said. 'I'm not on mains gas or electricity. And before you ask, yes, it does work out cheaper.'

Silcock drained his glass of water.

'Now, your call,' he said.

'Yes.'

I told him my story from the time that young Anna had tried to sell me a trick in Ramsden Lane, to visiting Naseem Khan, and then Anna being abducted by a couple of men.'

'If that's what happened,' Silcock said.

'It happened,' I said. 'She was with Mona, Malik's wife.'

'Malik? Your fat little Paki pal?'

'I see that you haven't attended that race awareness course, yet, Silcock.' I paused. 'There's no doubt she was snatched.'

'Unless she called them,' Silcock said. 'Gave them a bell, and went of her own free will.'

I admitted that I had not thought of that.

'But there's still the matter of her age. And her being trafficked from East Europe.'

'Tell me about it,' Silcock said.

'Meaning.....what?' I said.

'I mounted an operation last year when I learned that young women -'

'And children.'

'And children,' Silcock continued, 'were arriving from

Eastern Europe, Romania, Bulgaria, places like that. They are free to travel here, of course. This bloody European Union. But they are being brought over on false promises and pushed straight into working as whores.'

'Out on the streets of our once-fair city,' I said.

'And not just the streets.'

'You mean.....'

'I mean brothels,' Silcock said. 'Locked away. Drugged up. No chance of escape.'

Which was probably where Anna was right now, not to be trusted out on her own again.

'Do you remember the Charlene Downes case, Jack?'

This was the first time he had ever used my first name. It made a change from 'Cheeky bloody Yid.'

I shook my head.

'Fourteen year old kid. Seems she was being groomed for under-age sex.'

'Which punters like.'

'And not just the punters, Jack. The bastards who shelter young girls and get them hooked on drugs.'

'So what happened to Charlotte?'

'Charlene,' Silcock corrected me. 'She disappeared, presumed murdered. Two men were arrested and charged. A Jordanian and an Iranian.'

A memory came into my brain.

'And both were found Not Guilty,' I said.

'On appeal,' Silcock said sourly. 'And awarded two hundred and fifty quid compensation. Each. Both me ran takeaways and these are at the centre of grabbing kids for sex and prostitution. Especially in northern towns and cities.'

'What grounds.....what was the basis of their appeal?' I said.

'Technical irregularities in the way secret recordings were made. But we all know the real reason, don't we?'

'Because they are Muslims, that's why,' Silcock spat.

'Come on, Silcock,' I said, 'that can't be.......'

'It's true. Seems we don't want to upset social and community cohesion. It's getting harder and harder to gain a conviction where Pakistanis are involved.'

He paused. Picked up his glass, saw that it was empty, put it down again. I went to get a jug of cold water. Filled Silcock's glass. He slaked his thirst.

'By God, that water tastes good,' he said.

'No chlorine, no fluoride,' I said. 'Straight from a spring.'

'You get.......from a well?'

'Yes. But it's tapped in to the kitchen.'

'No gas, no water, no electricity. I'll bet you can't wait for candles to be invented. I'm surprised you don't get about on a donkey cart.'

'With the price of petrol what it is,' I said, 'that may well become an option.'

'There were rumours Charlene was put in a mincer, her body disposed of that way,' Silcock said.

'Probably made into kebabs,' I said.

'That's been rumoured as well,' Silcock said. 'Just thinking of it makes me sick.'; Hew looked me directly in the eyes. 'Tell me, Jack, doesn't just talking about this make you despair of human nature.'

I shook my head.

'I have no illusions about human nature,' I said. 'I've read many history books.'

'Yes, I can see them all lined up,' Silcock said, waving a hand toward my book shelves. 'How do you get to read them, if you've no electricity?' Then he said, 'Of course, the generator.'

'So what are you lot doing about child prostitution and abuse?' I said.

'Right now, nothing,' Silcock said. 'I flogged myself all hours of the day and most of the night, amassing evidence for a case, and when I was about ready, I was told to lay off.'

'The Crown Prosecution Service?' I said.

'I suppose so. But the news was handed down by the CC.'

'The Chief Constable?

'Sir Radley James Dickerson. In person. In his office. With no witnesses. Orders from the Big Dick himself.'

'Community cohesion?'

'If a Muslim crawled up his arse at dead of night and planted a bomb in his belly, he'd find as reason not to prosecute, the snivelling bastard.'

You know, Silcock, you can be quite poetic when the occasion takes you,' I said.

Silcock smiled, but it was a bitter smile.

'Forget about this kid, Jack. Hey! You didn't.......You like skirt, don't you?'

'Yes, but it has to be over sixteen,' I said.

'What type do you like particularly?'

'The type that breathes,' I said. 'I'm not yet into necrophilia.' And before he could speak, I said, "And I'm not going to forget it. There are some Augean stables in this town that need cleaning out.'

'And not just this town,' Silcock said. 'There's a cover up, and on a big scale. Political correctness gone mad. But not PC alone. Fear. Timidity. Do you know some of the kids are as young as eleven years old. All white girls, of course. Easy meat, fresh meat. And what do we do? Wee attend community forums to present information, carefully doctored info, of course. We talk to men at the mosques. We.......makes you laugh, doesn't it? - we try to raise awareness. The last time the Big Dick spoke on the subject, to the press, not in some mosque, and claimed we were making significant progress.'

By now I understood why Silcock had chosen to visit me at home.

'You're telling me to back off, aren't you?' I said.

Silcock nodded his head miserably.

'I wish I didn't have to.'

"I'll be wasting my time?'

'Any reports or complaints have to be passed immediately and directly to Dickerson himself.'

'And he sits on them,' I said.

'You catch on fast, Jack.'

'Not fast enough,' I said.

'What do you mean?'

'I mean,' I said, 'that I know full well I can't reform the whole rotten world, or even this stinking rotten town, but....'

'But?'

'I intend to rescue at least one child, one little girl, and get her back, if I can, to Lithuania.'

'Don't get involved, Jack,' Silcock warned me. 'These bastards won't think twice about putting you through a mincing machine, of one kind or another. And especially when they learn you are a Jew.'

'I am not a Jew,' I said harshly. 'I'm an atheist.'

'Don't get worked up,' Silcock said.

His stomach rumbled. We both heard it.

"You need something to eat, Mr Silcock,' I said.

He laughed. 'You got a bacon sandwich, Jack?'

I smiled back.

'Smoked or unsmoked? I can offer both.'

'You surprise me, Jack.'

'I told you. I am not a Jew.'

He followed me to the refrigerator in the kitchen.

'Be careful, Jack. These bastards have no scruples.'

'Me neither,' I said. 'Me neither.'

We ate the bacon sandwiches with tomato. Silcock asked for ketchup but I told him I don't but inessentials.

'Like you don't give any dosh to the utility companies,' he said.

We drank tea.

'I was thinking, when I retire, I might join your firm. What's the company called?'

'Jack Rubin, Associates,' I said.

'How many associates?'

'Just me and Malik,' I said.

'However,' Silcock said portentously, 'although my retirement isn't far off, I don't see you living so long.'

'That serious, is it?'

'You'd better believe it, boy.'

'Nobody calls me *boy*,' I said, snapping.

'OK, OK,' he said, and patted my shoulder. 'Get down off

that high horse.'

We went outside and stood by his car.

'One last thing,' I said. 'Can you give me a name? Off the record, and I won't even mention your name.'

'Not even to Malik,' he said.

'Especially not to him.'

Silcock drew in breath. 'I could just murder a ciggie,' he said.

'The name,' I said, my voice soft and persuasive.

'Zoltan. Sometimes calls himself Sultan. Zoltan Khan.'

'Any relation to.....'

'Naseem's brother. Or his cousin. These people, they are all related.'

Not related in the way we think, but of the same clan, perhaps. Malik might know.

Silcock got into his car and belted up. He opened the window.

'One last point, Sir.' He cleared his throat. 'I must hereby advise you not to undertake any action that might be deemed....'

'Illegal?' I said, and I laughed.

'I'll deny this meeting and disown you completely.'

'Support your local sheriff,' I said.

Silcock shook his head, as if in disbelief.

'I'll say this for you, Jack. You're a hard case. Nobody would ever guess you're a Yid.'

'Tell that to the Israeli Defence Force,' I said. 'Or Mossad.'

'I can imagine you in Mossad,' he said, and laughed immoderately.

He swung the car round and I heard his laughter as he drove away.

Chapter Eight

Certain parts of the city have become what are known locally as Asian areas. Going to these ghettos is like entering a foreign country. Such an area is Lakenwood.

Malik had discovered where Zoltan Khan lived. While he was doing that, I made a quick call to Ives. It had to be quick because the number I have is a cell phone and I didn't want to be racking up charges. I enquired if he had ever had dealings with Zoltan, and Ives was adamant he never had, and never would. He did not say why that should be. Both were well into drugs and prostitution, it seemed, but different areas, different tastes, and their operations did not overlap.

'Victoria Road?' I said, surprised. 'That's a run-down street, isn't it.'

'I drove down there, to check it out. Zoltan has made some alterations.'

'Without telling me? You sneaky little bugger,' I said.

'I used my initiative,' Malik said. 'I thought you'd be pleased.'

'I am. I'll make sure you get a bonus at the end of the year.'

'What about the end of the month?' he asked.

Well, there was no money coming in from this job. I know I am foolish to a degree but I had to see this matter of Anna through to the end, whatever that end may be. And I knew the end might well be my death, and maybe Malik with me. People who will feed a dead child into a meat mixer, if that is indeed what happened, will not hesitate to knock off a nosy member of the public. Which is what I was. I had no official standing, no connection with the police, no one. I was a stupid individual who had made it his business to rescue one child, and assuming she had returned to them voluntarily, a child who did not want to be rescued. It can't have been the sex, so it must have been the drugs. Far, far too many people know that drugs are killing them - after first destroying their nasal septum - but they cannot escape the craving.

Like methamphetamine. This is dangerous stuff, different from regular amphetamine pills. Without going into the chemistry, which in any case I do not fully understand, meth is simply a more refined or condensed form of amphetamine. It is much more powerful than most people know. It produces an intense feeling of energy and strong euphoric pleasure, both at the same time. Some of the intensity depends on how quickly it gets into the system. This drug in pill form, taken orally, is slow to produce an effect. Injecting it or smoking it, is a completely different experience. By smoking meth, large amounts of the drug can be dumped into the bloodstream, which is carried to the brain in a matter of seconds.

What does this feel like to the user? I don't know. I've never indulged. If silly buggers want to kill themselves, that's their business. But when kids are coerced into becoming addicts, that is another matter. In the real world, for most people, sex is perhaps the most pleasurable feeling possible. I'll not argue with that, except to add that there are other sensations, those of the brain, that are also intense and last longer. Meth users have said that it is like having one hundred orgasms all at once. I can only imagine.

'Malik.'

'Yes?'

Malik was switching on the kettle. Tea, on the hour, every hour.

'You've had experience with prostitutes.'

'So have you,' he said, sulkily.

'I'm not criticising you,' I said. 'What you do is your business.'

'Only once or twice,' he said defensively. 'And only when Mona was having a baby.'

'I understand. Take it easy,' I said. 'What I want to know is this. Which is most popular? Girls walking the streets? Or brothels?'

'How should I know?' he said, putting four teaspoons of sugar in his tea and copious amount of fresh milk, which he had purchased that morning on the way to the office.

'If I wanted to visit a brothel. Say....one in Lakenwood. How would I go about it?'

Malik shrugged his shoulders, almost spilled tea. As usual,

he had filled the mug to the brim.

'Don't be coy, Malik. This is important. For Anna's sake.'

'I think we should keep out of this,' Malik said.

'Why?'

'You don't mess with these people.'

'Are you afraid?' I said.

'You bet I am.'

I nodded my understanding.

'Then I'll keep you out of it,' I said. 'I mean, you have a wife and children.'

'Your mother's alive,' Malik said.

'Yes, but she doesn't remember me. My death wouldn't affect her,' I said.

'You don't have to die,' Malik said. 'Let's get back to making money.'

I could see his point. Every day I spent looking out for Anna was a day with no money going into the bank account.

'So answer my question,' I said.

'Which question?' Malik asked.

'I want to find a brothel -'

'In Lakenwood. Right! Well, you wait till after dark. Then you cruise along the streets. If a woman approaches you....'

'She'll be a police woman in mufti,' I said.

'She'll ask you what....what service you want. You ask her for prices. You agree on these. She hops into your car. She tells you where to go.'

'Can't I pick the spot?'

'She'll want a safe place, where people are watching out for her.'

'Her pimp?'

'Or another girl on the game,' Malik said. 'But if a man comes to your car....'

'Don't tell me he's a male prostitute. A bum boy.'

Malik smiled. 'You can find 'em, if that's what you want.'

'You know me, Watson. That's not what I want.'

'He'll ask you if he can help you. You tell him you're looking for something.....'

'Special?'

'Yes.'

'And eventually I admit that I'm looking for....'

'Fresh meat,' Malik said.

'And it doesn't have to be halal,' I said.

'Don't joke with this guy. He's out there in shop doorways and back alleys, but he's not just wandering about. He's a businessman. Probably one of Zoltan's men.'

I switched on the electric kettle. Still warm, the water soon boiled. I poured boiling water on to green tea leaves. No milk, no sugar. Green tea makes a change from my usual camomile.

'Let's go, Malik,' I said.

'Where?'

'Lakenwood. Where else?'

'But it isn't evening yet,' he protested.

'I just want to look round,' I said. 'Get the feel of the place.'

'It'll seem different after dark,' Malik said.

'I'm sure it will. But right now, my friend' – Malik loves it when I refer to him as *my friend* – 'right now it's broad daylight and I want to find my way around.'

Traffic lights, one-way streets, entrances and exits, that kind of thing. Like the Duke of Wellington, a man who fought and won many battles, said, it is important to know what is on the other side of the hill.

We went in Malik's battered Merc. He bought it cheap, boasted about what a bargain he had made, and then had to spend more than a coupled of thousand quid making it roadworthy. Malik's car did not stand out in Lakenwood; there were many Mercs parked outside houses.

Victoria Road was made up of late Victorian terrace houses. I was amazed they had avoided the developer's ball. Two places stood out. A shop that had formerly been about four houses had been developed into one Supermart. Outside, in what had been a garden, and on the pavement there were stalls crowded with fruit and vegetables. But what really stood out on that street was a large new house, very large.

'Zoltan's place,' Malik said.

'How the hell did he get planning permission?' I said. And added, 'And why am I asking such a stupid question?'

I told Malik to park up near Zoltan's house.

I could not take my eyes from the house. The stone, which was compound, was clean and bright, and contrasted starkly with the soot and grime of more than a century on other buildings. There was not a blade of grass to be seen; the front and sides of the house had been cleared for motor cars. Outside there were three motors: a Jeep, a Chelsea tractor, and a saloon car.

'What's the motor car, Malik?'

I'm not into cars as he is. To me, they are just lumps of metal to get me from one place to another without having to travel by bus or train.

'Subaru Impreza STI. New,' Malik said. '2.5 litre. Powerful.'

'Very nice,' I said. 'Very nice indeed.'

'I thought you didn't care about cars,' Malik said.

'I'm not talking about the bloody car,' I said. 'I mean the bird. That vision of delight across the road.'

Chapter Nine

A woman had emerged from a side door of the large house. She was dressed in traditional Asian gear, including the scarf covering her head. What was not covered was her face, and she was a doll. She carried a large black bag.

The key to the Subaru was electronic, of course. The woman eased herself gracefully into the driving seat. Switched on and drove out into the street, barely bothering to look left or right.

'Follow that car,' I said.

'What?'

'Follow the Subaru, you soft twat,' I said.

Malik is a very good driver. He followed the Subaru, being careful not to be spotted. As the woman carried a large black bag, I expected that she would be going in the direction of the town centre, just one mile down the road. I was surprised when she turned at the traffic lights and went in the opposite direction.

'Why are we following her?' Malik asked. 'Why are we wasting time? Tell me that, Mr Rubin.'

The woman was a looker, and no doubt. I could tell that

even when most of her was swathed in saris and ballooning trousers. I suspected that she might be Zoltan's relative, a sister, perhaps, or a cousin. That house in Victoria Road was large enough for an extended family. And I did not suppose a servant would be driving a top of the range Subaru. None of this was a good reason to follow her, but Malik and I had nothing better to do until nightfall, and what better way to beguile a few hours than to follow a nice-looking piece of skirt, although in there case there was no evidence of a skirt.

She went through the traffic lights down at Lakenwood Bar, past the old brewery on the right, and bore right. Malik followed, keeping one car between the Merc and the Subaru.

The road narrows where a large and imposing Victorian viaduct crosses the valley. Traffic has to slow down here at the best of times, but we were even slower today because of road works.

I saw the woman remove her head scarf. Black hair flowed down and across her shoulders. More to interest me, more to pull me in where I did not need to go.

Beyond the road works there was a lay by. She pulled into it, behind a large delivery van. There was no space for the Merc, even had we wanted to go in there.

'Keep going!' I said to Malik.

Because of the road works, the traffic was bunched together. Nevertheless, Malik signalled his intention to turn right, to make a U-turn.

'No!' I said. 'Keep going.'

75

He switched off the indicator and kept going forward I had been along this road before. There was a turning into a narrow steep hill, Station Road. Malik skilfully pulled in to the left, reversed, and was looking out from Station Road to the main road. We'd be able to see when the red Subaru, not a common car, went past.

When it did go past, crawling because of the heavy slow traffic, there was a surprise. The same woman was behind the wheel but she was dressed rather differently. She was wearing a white blouse that left her shoulders bare.

Malik's eyes popped out.

'Shit!' he said.

Given that he never swears or cusses, this was strong language, the expression of a powerful emotion.

Excrement was the last thing I'd have thought of.

'God! I could shag that,' I said aloud.

'And get your testicles cut off by Zoltan?' Malik asked.

He joined the line of traffic, now two cars behind the Subaru.

Malik never cussed and I never uttered the name of God. Both of us had broken a rule. That was the effect of the long black hair and brown bare shoulders of one young woman. I doubted that we were the only ones in that line of traffic consumed with lust.

Someone coming slowly in the other direction hooted his cart horn. The woman turned her head and flashed him a bright smile. A second man hooted and again was rewarded with that smile.

'She's lapping it up,' I said.

'The little tart,' Malik said.

'Yes,' I said, 'but you wouldn't kick her out of bed, would you?'

Two miles up the road, we came to a set of traffic lights. She signalled to go left.

'Which way?' Malik asked.

'Left,' I said.

'But she'll see us,' Malik protested.

'Left,' I said again. 'In for a penny, in for a pound.'

the Subaru opened up now because on this road there was no other traffic. Up the hill past the secondary school, past the entrance to the railway station – there's a whole series of small stations along this valley. Wee were leaving the valley, climbing the steeply to the hills above.

The young woman was now wearing sun shades. I doubted that she needed them; it was all part of the style package, the white blouse, bare shoulders, the long black hair. What was not in doubt was that she now knew we were following her, because when we reached the top of the hill, she signalled to go right and Malik did the same. Then, at the very last moment, swift enough to cause rubber to burn, she swung the Subaru to the left, and Malik followed suit. If she had wondered before, she was not wondering now.

She drove along a narrow winding road, on the edge of the hill's ridge. Top the right I could see Roman Hill. |It is a local landmark, standing high above the surrounding country. It is a place where people take their dogs to shit and to get exercise, and their children for the same reasons.

On the flat top of Roman Hill there is a monument to the Allied victory at Leipzig in 1813, the Battle of the Nations, a significant defeat for Napoleon Bonaparte. If the locals had waited two years, they could have commemorated the Battle of Waterloo, Wellington's famous victory.

There is a narrow road to the top of the hill and a paved area for parking cars. It was to the top of Roman Hill that we followed the Subaru.

Our female friend was in no hurry to get out. She seemed to be fiddling with something inside the car. When, finally, she emerged it was clear enough that she had been arranging her clothing. In place of the woman in the Muslim gear she had been wearing when she left Victoria Road was a modern bird in mini skirt, white blouse and black high heeled shoes.

'Jee-zus,' Malik said.

'Too bloody true,' I said.

The woman half looked at us over her shoulder and then started to walk as fast as her shoes would take her, which wasn't very fast, toward the monument.

I clapped my hands together. I opened the car door.

'Where are you going?' Malik asked anxiously.

'Make one intelligent guess,' I said.

'No, please, Mr Rubin, no.'

There was genuine concern in his voice.

I wasn't listening.

I can resist most things but temptation is not one of the things. Show me a pretty young woman, or even an attractive one who is not so young – and this one was the former, in so far as I could tell – and I lose my common sense, my sense of danger.

'I quickly caught up with her.

'Hi!' I held out my hand. 'My name's Jack.'

She did not accept the handshake.

She pulled the blouse higher on her shoulders but not before I'd had a good view of her large and generous tits.

'What do you want?' she asked coldly.

She shivered a little.

'It's always cold up here on Roman Hill,' I said. 'You should have brought a cardigan.

'I come here to enjoy the stillness, the silence. And you... you....'

'I only want to be friendly,' I said.

'Are you police?'

'No way. Do I look like a copper?'

'Yes.'

'I'll try to change that,' I said.

'Are you a stalker, then?'

'No,' I said, and treated her to a broad smile. 'Do I look like a stalker?'

She shrugged and I had a flash of nipple. The areolar tissue was brown, almost black. This bird had given birth to a chick.

'I had a stalker once,'she said. 'Everywhere that I went, he followed me.'

'Well, I don't see him right now. His day off, is it?'

'It's been his day off for some time. Ever since my husband …..ever since he..... scrted him out.'

'Why don't we walk round the hill?' I said. 'I know the history. For a start, it was never a Roman hill. It belonged to a tribe called the Brigantes. They had a queen. Cartimandua. Quite a girl, I believe.'

'Please go away, Mr......'

'Rubin. Jack Rubin.' Local historian and all-round good guy.'

She laughed.

'Tell me about this monument,' she said.

'Hang on,' I said. 'I'm at a disadvantage. You know my name but I -'

'Kavita,' she said. 'It's a Kashmiri name.'

'Kavita,' I said. 'A very attractive name for a very attractive young woman.'

'My husband likes it,' she said, seeking to put the kybosh

on our nascent relationship.

'And my husband's name is -'

'Don't tell me,' I said. 'Let me guess.' I paused, pretending to think. 'It wouldn't, by any chance, be Khan, would it? Zoltan Khan.'

'You know damn well it is,' she said, and the venom in her voiced quite spoiled the attractiveness of her face.

'Zoltan would not be happy if he knew you'd followed me up here.'

'And I suspect he wouldn't be overjoyed if he knew you were flaunting your body in a public place. Though I must say, the gear suits you. Better than that shalwar kameez on the back seat of the Subaru.'

She had no answer, or not one she chose to share with me.

'OK, Kavita. Why don't I give you that tour of Roman Hill, and explain why the monument was built.'

'I have another suggestion,' she said, and treated me to the mother of all smiles.

If she had suggested us coupling, there behind the monument to the Battle of the Nations, I'd have accepted like a shot. But she didn't.

'What's your suggestion, Kavita?'

'Mr Rubin, why don't you piss off?'

With that she strode back to the Subaru as fast as her heels would allow.

I went over to the Merc. Malik looked anxiously at me. As well he might.

'Is it?'

I nodded. 'Mrs Zoltan Khan.'

'Now we're really in deep trouble,' Malik said morosely.

'Maybe yes, and maybe no,' I said.

'Did you make any....headway?' he said.

'Not exactly.'

Malik permitted himself a worried smile.

'I thought you could pull any bird you wanted.'

'I usually can.'

'So what went wrong this time?'

'She must be a lesbian,' I said.

Chapter Ten

I rose early. Told myself it was a shame not to enjoy the dawn and the warm sun afterwards. The truth was, my mind was a maelstrom. My sleep had been agitated and sporadic. Yet I awoke feeling fit, even refreshed.

By seven o'clock the sun was warm on my face. There was no suggestion of the keen breeze to be found on the hills early in the morning, even in Summer.

I walked round my plot. There is little grass; the place is too high for that. The person who lived here before me had tried to do something with the land, but even when I purchased the cottage it was clear he had failed. Now the whole plot – you can't call it a garden – has reverted to bog grass. And sedge. Don't be fooled – sedges may resemble grass and rushes, but they are quite separate. They grow on wet and poor soil, where nothing else will grow. I often feel that sedges and I have a lot in common.

After about ten minutes I went inside to prepare breakfast. No problems there: porridge oats, which had soaked throughout the night, followed by a two-egg omelette, with onions and a tomato cut into small pieces.

Some Saturdays I go into the office but today was going to be the complete rest I had been promising myself for some time. I didn't want telephone calls, I didn't want to see Malik. My aim was to chill out all weekend.

Sounds idyllic and in some respects it was, but there was nothing peaceful about my brain. I had decided that the best way to catch a hornet was to stir up its nest. Sure, I might get stung in the meantime, but the hornet would end up squashed flat.

It was not a plan. It was a way of working. Make things happen. Keep the other guy on his toes. Except the toes I'd trodden on were those with painted nails, the toes of the hornet's wife. Given that Kavita had been cavorting in public in mini skirt that showed lots of leg, which most assuredly aint Muslim tradition, and that she had been wearing a thin blouse that left very little to the imagination – and I have a rampant imagination – I guessed that she might not deem it wise to report the Roman Hill meeting to her husband.

Make things happen. Blunder in. But not with the Boss's wife. That had not been any part of a plan, no matter how ill-formed. I had instructed Malik to follow the Subaru because the woman driving attracted me. I was s till without a plan for rescuing Anna, but I knew full well what I'd like to do with the delectable Kavita.

Idylls don't last long. This one didn't. I heard the vehicle before it arrived near my front door. It was a taxi. I had not ordered a taxi. But my visitor had.

I sighed. It was Malik and Mona. Good people, both, but I had wanted to be completely alone for a couple of days. Quite apart from anything else, I had a lot of thinking to do. What would be best for Anna, when I found her again? How could I bring some pain and discomfort to that bastard Zoltan Khan, lording it over his neighbours in a house that screamed dirty deeds and ill-gotten money?

I greeted Mona, hiding my true feelings behind a mask. There's no art to find the mind's construction in the face, the old king said, and I hoped it was true as I smiled at Mona. She did not return my smile. her face was lined with worry.

Malik paid off the taxi driver but only after a short discussion that suggested the driver was charging over the odds. In this city all taxi drivers are of Pakistan family origin, with perhaps a few Bengalis, and Malik's origins in Punjab did not protect him.

Business done, Malik hurried over to where I waited with Mona. She was crying by now, soft tears falling down her face, no sobbing, no hysteria, just gentle tears.

Malik and I shook hands. I could tell something had made him agitated.

I motioned Mona into the house.

'Make yourself a cup of tea, Mona,' I said.

She nodded.

'Coffee for me,' Malik said. Then, 'Let's talk outside, Mr Rubin.'

We went outside into the morning sunshine, and walked among the sedge and bog grass. Insects rose and whirred.

'So, Malik, what is it?'

'The Merc,'he said.

'Broken down again, has it?'

I did not smile. I could tell he was troubled. His shoulders heaved with emotion and his jowls were a match for S. Z. Sakall. You remember him: Cuddles. Carl the head waiter in Casablanca.

'The middle of the night,' he said. 'They torched the Merc.'

'They?' I said quietly, and even as I spoke the word I could feel something bitter gnawing at my entrails.

'Mona saw the flames first. She woke me. We got the boys into the back garden.'

'Where are the boys now?'

'With my brother and his family. What are we going to do? Malik asked.

'We're going to go inside, drink that coffee. I think I have some biscuits. Custard creams.'

'Your favourites,' Malik said.

It's at moments of tension that we rely on commonplace comments, and tension was evident in Malik's voice.

We went inside.

Mona sat on the sofa.

'You look tired, Mona,' I said.

'We did not sleep much last night,' she said, in her careful

English.

I suggested she kip down in the spare room, the one that Anna had slept in. Luckily, I had washed and changed the bedding. Mona needed no persuasion.

I sat down outside with Malik.

'We went to bed after midnight. It must have been about two when Mona disturbed me. Shortly after, the fire brigade arrived. A neighbour must have called them.'

Malik was not keeping his narrative in order.

'What wakened Mona?' I said. 'Why'd the fire brigade come?'

'I told you,' he said, giving me a look of reproach. 'They torched the Merc.''It was parked out in the street,' I said.

'In the front. The fire officer – e said the way it had blazed-'

'Doused with petrol,' I said.

'The police arrived. Kept me talking fore three hours.'

'You must also be tired,' I said.

'I am. They wanted to know if I'd upset my neighbours. Did I have any enemies. That kind of thing. Making notes in pencil.' Saying the same things over and over again to different people.'

'So you never got any sleep last night,' I said.

'I didn't tell the police anything,'Malik said.

'About Anna, and Zoltan Khan?'

'Never mentioned it,' Malik said. 'I suppose it was Zoltan.'

'Very likely,' I said.

'One copper, a sergeant, he said it was probably a race thing.'

'Racially motivated,' I said.

'That's exactly what he said.'

'That's what the bastards always say.' I shook my head. 'I expected Zoltan to come after me. I didn't guess he'd have a go at you.'

'And that isn't all,' Malik said.

He fished in the pocket of his jacket and took out a piece of paper. A half page torn clumsily from a kid's exercise book.

Someone had written, using a ball point pen – they were clearly three steps in advance of the police in terms of writing equipment – in childish capital letters:

NEXT TIME ITS THE HOUSE.'

'There's an apostrophe missing,' I said.

'What?'

'Never mind,' I said. And asked, 'Did you show this to the cops?'

'Should I have done?'

I shook my head. 'No.'

I drained my cup of coffee. Mona had made it in a cup, with a saucer, and I prefer a mug.

I ate two biscuits and decided to double the number. I'm a sucker for custard creams – and for good-looking women, of course. You know, if I had to choose between custard creams and women, if there were no other choice, I would choose.....women! I may like biscuits, but I'm not a pillock entirely.

'So what do we do now?' Malik said.

The look on his face was accusatory. I'd landed him into this. It was my job top get him out. That they meant what they had written – next time, the house – I did not for one moment doubt. We were dealing with unpleasant and murderous bastards. Anyone who hooks kids on drugs and then puts them out as meat for depraved punters, belongs to a different species from the rest of us. Arson is not as uncommon as you might think, at least among certain segments of our socially cohesive nation. Social cohesion? Lick my arse!

It was decided that we would allow Mona to sleep. I offered the sofa to Malik but he declined. He wanted to be awake, alert, and not too far from what he hoped was my protection. Later, when it was dark, Mona would stay with Malik's brother and his family, where the boys already were. Then Malik would return with me to the moorland cottage.

As I drove the Volvo back home that evening at about ten o'clock, I felt hungry. We stopped at a takeaway. I hoped it wasn't one of the more than fifty takeaways in the city that had recently been identified by health and safety people as having rats and cigarette butts all over the kitchen floor. I had a bigger worry - that in my absence someone had torched my place. It was a needless worry

We ate our food, Malik like a wolf; he had cleared his plate before I had even torn my naan bread into pieces. I opened a bottle of red wine. I could tell Malik wanted a glass.

'Have some,' I said. 'Be like me. I don't worry about kosher or unclean animals, or any of that Mosaic shit. They say red wine is good for your blood. That may not be true. It is alcoholic, though, but mildly.'

'Give me a glass,' Malik said with a vigour belying the fact he had not slept in the past twenty-odd hours, and not much before that.

He downed the wine in one gulp.

'Take it easy,' I said. 'Savour the grape.'

He sipped gently.

'What next?' he said.

I also drank wine.

'We get a good night's kip,' I said. 'We look at our options. Tomorrow. We plan our campaign.'

'We have a....a campaign?' Malik said.

'No, we don't,' I said, and laughed. 'That's why first of all we are going to go down to Lakenwood, on to Victoria Road, and torch -'

'His house?' Malik said, horrified.

'Not yet,' I said. 'Not unless we have to.'

'Then what?'

'We....' I paused for dramatic effect.....then we torch Kavita's Subaru Impreza.' And added, with venom in my voice, 'STI. 2-5 litre.'

Tired though he was, Malik's eyes opened wide with surprise and with something akin to delight.

'Is that halal enough for you, Mr Malik. Is it?' I said fiercely.

He nodded, drank more red wine, and fell asleep, there on the settee, filly clothed. I removed his shoes, loosened his tie, placed a blanket over him and went to my bedroom. I closed the door of my room. I did not want to hear Malik's snoring.

I lay in bed, and for the first time since Anna had stuck her head in my car window – how long ago it all seemed – my mind was clear, my brain no longer in tumult. The very notion of torching the Subaru turned me on. As did the Subaru's owner. But if I wanted to set Kavita on fire, it would have to be with something more personal than cans of petrol.

Chapter Eleven

'Revenge is a dish best eaten cold,' I said.

'Shakespeare?' Malik asked.

'No.'

'You?'

'I wish,' I said, and smiled. 'I used to think it was Francis Bacon, but now I'm not sure.'

'Bacon?' Malik sat up straight. 'We had a teacher at school. Said Bacon wrote Shakespeare's plays.'

'Your teacher was wrong. Shakespeare wrote Shakespeare's plays.'

Both Malik and I knew that we were avoiding the real subject. The burning of Mrs Kavita Khan's sparkling new red Subaru. Impreza.

Malik had suggested rushing off and doing this, that and the other, and I was able to remind him that we would be leaving behind a trail of evidence that even a novice in the CID would be able to trace, even with a blindfold over his eyes.

'You mustn't be seen to be involved. You need an alias for

the time I light the fire.'

'But I want to help,' Malik said. 'It was my Merc they torched.'

'And so you'll be the first to feel police hands on your collar,' I said.

I persuaded Malik that the best thing for him was to establish man alibi so firm that not even the cops would be able to break it down. He accepted what I suggested. Stay with his brother and sister-in-law. Never go out. Watch television and remember what he watched. The police were certain to question him and I would not be there to help so it was essential that he told the truth.

'You will be suspect number one,' I said.

'And you'll be number two,' he said.

I knew that, just as certainly as I knew that I'd be better able to withstand police pressure than he was.

I warned him that the police would use scare tactics. They would charge him; he would be found guilty – but if he were to confess, he might get away lightly. And if he refused to believe those threats, they would offer him a deal – deliver up Jack Rubin, and they would drop all charges relating to him.

'I'll never betray you, Mr Rubin,' he said earnestly.

'Do I hear a cock crowing three times?'

'What?'

'Nothing important,' I said.

He asked me when I would do the job and I told him it could be that very night, or the next night. I had to purchase petrol cans and fill them with petrol.

'I have two cans at home,' he said. 'You can have them.'

'Malik. Don't you ever listen?

His face clouded over. I told him that we must not have any contact, there must be nothing that tied him to me in regard to this attack on Zoltan Khan. Information could not be confided. I would not contact him at all. The following day we would both turned up at the office, separately. There was to be no mention of my activities in the small hours.

'And most important of all, Malik. No telephone calls. Use your mobile to telephone Pakistan. Do that round about midnight. How far behind us is Pakistan?'

'They're five hours in front,' Malik said.

And I always thought they were about five hundred years behind.

'The police will treat this seriously. They will come knocking. They will categorise it as a racial attack. Only you and I know the truth. So don't admit to anything. Don't answer questions they don't ask. As I said, do not listen to blandishments.'

'What?'

'Promises. Offers. They will be traps.'

'Right.'

'And under no circumstances refer to this to your family.

94

Not even Mona. Not your brother. If they know nothing better for them.'

Malik nodded his head, to indicate his agreement.

'No mention of it in a phone call or a text message. You got that?' I said. 'I'll see you tomorrow morning in the office. And don't even mention it then or ask questions. Important, that.'

'Do you think the office is bugged?' Malik asked.

'It wouldn't surprise me,' I said. 'We probably all have listening devices up our arses.'

I drove Malik to within about a mile of the town centre. I ordered him to catch a bus, keep the ticket, look up at the CCTV camera installed in the bus, but never to look at it anxiously.

As he opened the car door he asked if he could go out. I told him he could but preferably as a family. Go to the cinema, and retain the ticket stub. Or go with his brother and sister-in-law to a supermarket – lots of CCTV cameras there – and be sure also to keep the receipt. In short, establish in as many ways as possible that he was nowhere near Lakenwood.

He slammed the car door shut. Then stuck his head in the open window.

'Good luck, Mr Rubin,' he said.

'There is no such thing as luck, Mr Malik. Now.. ..go!'

I drove for about ten miles, found a DIY store, parked, went inside, purchased a petrol can – plastic, of course, like everything else, these days – and paid in cash. Then I drove

95

about eight miles to a supermarket, and went through the same routine again. I hoped two cans would be enough.

I drove toward the motorway and five miles to the nearest service station, where I filled the first can with petrol and again used cash to pay. There are CCTV cameras at service stations so I did not waste time.

My next stop was a small filling station on the way home. When I arrived, it was busy. This pleased me – there was less chance that the staff would remember me. I did not talk to the girl who took my money. I did not look up either; keeping one's head down makes it harder to be identified on the camera playback.

Once at the cottage, I took out the cans and placed them in an outhouse to the rear of the property. I opened all four doors of the Volvo, to clear the car of petrol fumes.

I took a shower and went to bed. I set the alarm for eleven o'clock. I needed to bed awakened. I was on the night shift.

Chapter Twelve

What did I hope to achieve?

Revenge, certainly; I have mentioned that. Revenge for the unwarranted attack on Malik's Mercedes Benz.

But also, in foolish and quixotic way, freedom fcr Anna, striking a blow for children everywhere who are being held captive and forced to perform sexual acts for bad bastards who like to use children. Foolish and quixotic because I have no desire to improve the world and no illusions about being able to smash this rotten trade in human flesh. Prostitution isn't known as the oldest trade for no reason and if women want to sell themselves for drugs or a packet of cigarettes, I'm not going to try and stop them. Burning Kavita's car was no going to save the world or even the exploited children of this city. But it was one step on the road to rescuing Anna.

Did she deserve to be rescued? After all, she had called for her keepers to take her from Malik's house, right under Mona's nose. The lure of drugs had proved stronger than the value of freedom from exploitation. Of course she deserved to be rescued. It was not a matter of what she wanted, or thought she wanted; it was a matter of what I deemed best for her.

So did I fancy her myself? I had asked this question right from the beginning, and been honest with myself. I did not wish to have sex with a child, even if she were willing. Had that been the case, I could have taken her while she was staying at my place, in the spare room.

Here's a statement. I, Jack Rubin, believe in nothing. I am as much a nihilist as it is possible to be. Good and evil I consider to be social constructs. Right and wrong are merely convenient ways to maintain some semblance of order in society. I have no religion, no political beliefs. I do not want to change or improve the world, because I think that is an impossible task. I trust very few. There is only one animal in the hole world to fear, and that is the human animal, savage, nasty, murderous, fashioned by evolution but with a defective gene. Good deeds are for do-gooders and soft liberals, little old ladies who give money to Christian Aid and cannot believe that their mite is given tom terrorists who use it to purchase arms, and who consider those little old ladies to be useful idiots.

So why me and Anna? Had things been different, had I married young, had we had a child, and if that girl had been a girl, she would perhaps be about fourteen years old. You can accuse me of being corny and soppy – which I'd deny – but that's the best and most honest answer that I can give. Anna could have been my own child, and for a child of mine I would maim, fight, scratch, and, if need be, kill.

Whenever I sleep, I dream. Even if it is only a cat nap, I dream. What my dream was that late evening I cannot remember, but I remember it seemed deep, and when the sound of the alarm clock cut into it, I sat bolt upright in bed.

I did not lie down again, lest I should fall asleep. I took another shower. I ate porridge. Then I dressed. Not my usual gear, but a pair of old overalls I had found in the outhouse and which I had not worn for some years.

I had already laid out five black waste bags. One for a change of clothing, and two each to cover the petrol cans. I did not want the pervasive smell of petrol to linger in the motor, so double-bagging was the order of the day – or night, as that should be.

By the time I had completed all my preparations, it was one o'clock in the morning. I placed the bagged petrol cans in the back of the car. The boot was too obvious a place. Also, I wanted my deed to be swift, clean and short. No time to hang about and grin contentedly as the Subaru went up in flames.

I know this town like the back of my hand. I had already decided on my route. The back roads, where cameras were unlikely to be in evidence.

I was driving steadily up Owl Ing road to the top of a hill. I reached the flat plateau. It was as quiet as death up there. Even the large hilltop hotel and restaurants had few lights on. I smiled. Down the hill at the other side, across the river and the canal in Millbridge, up another hill, that used to called Pinfold, but now has a more contemporary name. In medieval times the name Pinfold was given to the area where stray cattle were kept until their owners forked out a fine for their return. Not many animals in this area now, and not much grass; the only animals in this part of the city are human animals.

You will remember in all those old war films, the ones

99

where daring men plot to escape, and before they break out of the tunnel the escape officer always says something about checking one last time, because there is always something one has forgotten, something obvious perhaps, something necessary.

I was smiling happily as I let the Volvo free-wheel down Scar Edge Road. Not many lights there either, not at this time of the morning. It would not be long before I reached Lakenwood, stopped in Victoria Road, near to Zoltan Khan's place, and.........

Shit! And shit again!" I had forgotten the one necessary item. Something to ignite the petrol. I put the car in gear and pulled up at the side, where the road crosses the railway. I was a number one, first-class, egregious twat.

After a couple of minutes I drove off in the direction of town. As I was driving down Manchester Road I saw a garage that was open. I sighed with relief. Everything was in my favour. These all-night places get knocked off by thieves so they do not mallow customers in the shop during the small hours. Payment is through a window with thick reinforced bullet-proof glass.

The guy in the shop looked tired, as well he might. He probably drove a taxi during the day and hoped to get some sleep during the night.

Many smokers believe that roll-your-own cigarettes are not as harmful as manufactured cigarettes. Many smokers change to smoking roll-ups rather than stop smoking in the mistaken belief that they will smoke less tobacco and inhale fewer toxic chemicals. This is wrong; hand-rolling tobacco is as just as harmful as the tobacco in manufactured cigarettes. Research using roll-up cigarettes made by smokers, shows that the levels of nicotine and cancer-causing chemicals inhaled are often higher than those from bought cigarettes. Such cigarettes are more likely to cause mouth, throat and lung cancer as well as lung diseases such as emphysema and heart disease.

But I wasn't going to smoke. Buying tobacco as well as lighters was a deception.

Golden Virginia and two BIC lighters,' I said hoarsely to the window.

'Packs of five,' the guy said.

'Sure.'

I handed over my money and walked back to the Volvo.

I turned back up the main road, left at Pinfold, over the top again – this is a city of many hills – and down into Lakenwood and Victoria Street.

I drove down the road, checking to see if there were security guards. The Subaru was there, but the gates to the front of the house were open. Zoltan must have felt confident that his status in the community made him immune from theft. That's as may be. What he was not immune from, this night, was arson.

So far, so good! Now, however, I was at my most vulnerable. I had to park the Volvo near to Zoltan's house so that I might not spend too much times carrying the petrol cans. I drove slowly and quietly and parked on the other side of the street. I opened the door but did not close it fully, let along slam it. I opened the back door, driver's side, and took out both petrol cans.

I wasted no time, poured both cans of petrol over the

Subaru. I looked up and listened. No sounds, no even an owl hooting in the night.

The next bit was potentially dangerous. That was why I had brought with me newspapers. They were already screwed up. I lit one, let the flame take hold, and threw it at the Subaru, I was in luck: flames spread quickly.

No time to stand and stare. I sprinted back to the car, closed the rear door as quietly as possible, and got behind the wheel. I pulled away quickly. and by the time I had reached the Supermart further along Victoria Road I heard a loud explosion. The petrol tank had blown.

No time to waste, but nor was this the time to drive like a lunatic and draw attention to myself. I knew what I had planned. Once in Millbridge I turned right into George Street and drove on to the end, where the river runs through an industrial area.

I kept the engine running while I got out and removed the boiler suit. I placed it in the black bag, drew the strings at the top, and slung the bag as far as I could into the middled of the river, where the flow was strongest. The tobacco and the two lighters followed after. Even if they were recovered, there was little likelihood of fingerprints.

Now, dressed in dark trousers and a dark green tee shirt, I drove back to the cottage. About one mile from home, I took off my shoes and threw them far from the road and into a small tarn, where they sunk into the water.

Yet another shower, and I was in bed. I fell asleep almost at once.

It was six o'clock in the morning when I was awakened by

a loud banging on the front door and on the windows I smiled. I was expecting this. I put on my dressing gown, which I rarely use in the warm months, and went toward the front door, just as it was knocked down by a battering ram.

Outside, lights from three police vehicles flashed urgently.

'The door wasn't locked,' I said.

A gloved hand, bunched into a hard fist, struck me full in the face.

After that, I said nothing. Mainly because of the blood pouring from my lips and mouth.

Chapter Thirteen

'Still causing trouble, then, eh, Rubin?'

'Hello, David.'

Dave Lunn and I had joined at the same time. Actually, he was three months ahead of me and never allowed me to forget it, although he went quiet when I passed the first exams and he had to re-sit.

'So now you've added wilful arson to your list of crimes.'

'Sorry,' I said, as innocently as I could manage.

'Don't come the old soldier with me, Rubin. We have witnesses.'

I almost smiled. Whatever else Lunn had, he did not have witnesses; I'd covered my tracks too well for that – at least I hoped that I had.

'If you tell me, Dave, why I'm sitting here, cuffed, and I haven't a clue -'

Dave Lunn moved faster than I would have expected for a man who had put on weight. One minute he was sitting opposite me, and the next he was on my side of the table, and thumping me around the chest. At least he had learned not to strike a prisoner on the face or the head, where it showed.

Being handcuffed, I could not defend myself.

When Lunn had finished bashing me – something he had probably wanted to do from the first day we met, and certainly when I passed the exams and he failed all his first time – he rubbed his hands together and went to sit down again. By this time I was on the floor. Lunn made no attempt to help me back to my chair and there was no way, absolutely no way, I was going to ask him for assistance.

After a bit of a struggle, I was again sitting down. I knew damn well he would not have dared to take me on in an equal contest, me without handcuffs, but I resisted the temptation to tell him that.

'If you could tell me what this is all about, Dave?'

'Detective Sergeant Lunn to you, Rubin. Detective Sergeant Lunn. And don't you forget it.'

All these years and he had not risen above sergeant, and with his academic record and general low intelligence had done rather well to get so high. I would not have trusted the little shit to walk straight.

'Right, Detective Sergeant. Perhaps you'd care to enlighten me. Why was I disturbed from my beauty sleep -'

'Beauty?' he interrupted, laughing coarsely. 'You'll never be beautiful, Rubin. No Yid ever is.'

'Tell that to Goldie Hawn. Natalie Portman. Gwyneth Paltrow.'

I could tell from the glazed look on Lunn's face that the trivia of movies was not an interest of his.

'And why am I here? Handcuffed.'

'Arson, that's why,' Lunn said.

'Arson?'

Again I had to sound innocent and yet make it sound convincing.

'A serious charge,' he said.

'If it's serious, why have they given it to a lowly detective sergeant?' I said, and immediately regretted my words.

Lunn reached over and switched on a recording machine. He looked down at a sheet of paper. He is so thick he cannot even remember the order of words.

'It is my duty to warn you, Mr Rubin, that you have the right to remain silent -'

'Cut that out, Dave. Just tell me what this is all about.'

He switched off the machine.

'Arson. My case. I don't know what the hell you're talking about.'

'Where were you last night between the hours of midnight and when our cars called round at your place?'

'In bed. And your lot woke me up.'

'No,' Lunn said. 'That's a lie. You were in Victoria Street, in Lakenwood. Setting fire to a motor vehicle, a Subaru Impreza, registration number....'

He started to search through the sheaf of papers but could not find the one with the Subaru's registration number.

I remained silent. Let him flounder. I could feel the pain in my chest where he had thumped me but I have known worse pain; Dave Lunn is hardly a man whom is good with his fists. However, I am good with my fists, given the chance, and I vowed to get a measure of revenge when the time was right. As I had told Malik, revenge is a dish best eaten cold.

We pussyfooted for about thirty minutes - at least, he did - never quite getting round to reading me my Miranda, as the Americans call it, and not feeling confident enough to charge me, bang me in a cell, and allow me to contact my solicitor, as if I ever would. Lunn's interrogation skills were of a low order; had our roles been reversed, I'd have had him pleading guilty to all manner of crimes, and would never have laid a finger on him. There are better forms of persuasion than fisticuffs.

At last, I decided that I had had enough. My wrists were chafed by the handcuffs – the ratchet type that tighten if one tries to struggle free. Lunn bored the arse off of me. And I was feeling desperately tired, but did my best to restrain myself from yawning; I didn't want Lunn to guess I'd been up half the night dousing the Subaru with unleaded petrol.

'What time is it, Dave?' I said.

Truth to tell, Lunn looked as tired as I felt. There were no windows in that interrogation room and no clocks either.

'Where you're going, time won't matter,' he said, and attempted a smile which emerged more like baby wind than merriment.

'The only place I am going, Dave' – he had stopped insisting I refer to him by rank and surname – 'is home, to catch up on the kip you buggers disturbed. So....either charge me, or release me.'

'We have the right to hold you for....'

He did not finish the sentence. He could not remember how long he had the right to hold me there, and in any case those decisions were going to be made by people higher up the food chain. As far as responsibility and decisions were concerned, Dave Lunn was definitely a bottom feeder.

I stood up.

'I'll repeat, Dave. Charge me or release me. Charge me and it'll never get to court.'

'Why not?'

'Lack of evidence, that's why. And when you release me I'll be considering compensation for wrongful arrest, from the county force in general, and for assault by you in particular.'

'Now wait a minute, Jack.'

Suddenly I was Jack.

I held out my arms, willing him to take off those bloody awful cuffs.

He did not do so.

'Wait here,' he said.

Stupidly. Where was I going to go, restrained at the wrists?

When Lunn returned, he was not alone. He was accompanied by Chief Superintendent Silcock.

Silcock glowered at me.

'What's your name, son?'

'Jack Rubin,' I said.

'Sir!' he barked.

And he stepped forward and hit me hard in the belly. Not enough force to drop me, but I went down nevertheless.

'Jackis Rubin, Sir,' I said.

'On your feet, lad,' Silcock said, and he helped me up. 'Now sit down and answer all questions truthfully.'

I sat down.

Silcock looked at Lunn.

'Take off the cuffs, Dave,' he ordered. 'And get yourself a bite to eat.'

'Sir?'

'Go and have some breakfast, for God's sake,' Silcock ordered.

Lunn removed the handcuffs. I resisted the temptation to rub my feeling back into my wrist joints. Worst thing I could do was break the skin.

Lunn left the room and was clearly pleased to do so. Once the door was closed, Silcock looked at me.

'Sorry about that,' he said.

'Thumping me in the gut?'

'Yes. I had to make it look good for Lunn.'

'I never felt a thing,' I said. 'You must be losing your touch.'

Silcock grinned.

'So you went round to Khan's house and burned his wife's car.'

'Is that what Dave Lunn was talking about?' I said. 'He kept mumbling something about arson.'

'Come off it, Jack. It was you, wasn't it?'

I smiled. I was not born yesterday, and did not trust Silcock.

'I went to bed early, read a book till midnight, and then slept well until your goons woke me at about five o'clock this morning.'

'What book did you read in bed? Wankers' Annual?'

'How much did you subscription cost you, Silcock?' I said. 'If you must know, I was reading about Arthur Schopenhauer.'

'Who the hell is he?' Silcock asked, as I guessed he would.

'He was a German philosopher,' I said.

'Makes interesting reading, does he?' Silcock sneered.

'He's different from all other major philosophers, because he was a pessimist.'

'Was he like you? A Yid.'

I ignored the provocation.

'I have to get home,' I said. 'I'm tired.'

'You must be,' Silcock smiled. 'Having been up all night burning motor cars.'

I almost reminded him that it was only one motor car but I remembered in time.

I yawned.

'I'll get a car to take you home,' Silcock said.

'Your kindness is well-known in the force,' I said.

'So long as you promise not to burn it.'

We walked down to the cars. Silcock signed a chitty.

He spoke to the driver. I could not hear what was being said.

'I was about to get in the car when Dave Lunn burst out into the parking area.

'What's going on here, Mr Silcock?'

'What's going on here, Dave, is that this man is being released for lack of evidence.' Lunn's disappointment showed on his face. 'Now go back and finish your breakfast,' Silcock said, 'and remove that egg from your tie.'

Lunn's right hand went immediately to where his tie should have been, and then he remembered that he wasn't wearing a tie, and he had not yet eaten an egg. Lunn looked disconcerted and foolish, and Silcock laughed loudly.

'Pillock,' Silcock said quietly. And then, even quieter still, he said to me, so that even the driver could not hear,

'Jack! Try the Kashmir takeaway in Chapel Hill.'

Chapter Fourteen

'Mr Malik.'

'Mr Rubin,' Malik said.

'I think you know me by now,' I said.

Malik shook his head and his jowls wobbled.

'I don't think I will ever know you,' he said.

I switched on the electric kettle. A Russell Hobbs I have had for years.

I did not respond to Malik's comment.

'You are the strangest man I have ever met,' he said. And added, 'No sugar for me.'

'No...sugar? And you have all those adipose cells to feed?' I paused. 'And in any case, you know the rule in this office. We make our own drinks. We always drink from out own mugs. I don't want your syphilitic lips on my china.'

'That is what I mean.' Malik said. 'Always insulting me like that. You are intelligent, Mr Rubin, but very, very stupid.'

'Cut the compliments.' I said, removing the tea bag from my mug.

I'd get another three or four drinks out of that tea bag.

No milk, no sugar, no caffeine. Straight camomile or, on this occasion, lemon and ginger. Sainsbury's best.

I looked out of the window on to the square below. The layout of the square of the square has been changed. The local authority has no notion of what ism attractive and less idea of how to keep costs down. Where once there were flower beds, now there are large paving stones, imported from China or Vietnam. A back-hander for someone in there, somewhere. Fountains play and it all looks very silly.

'They've been very quiet, Malik.'

'Planning something,' he said, and looked worried.

'Perhaps you should go away,' I said. 'You and the wife. Keep quiet until this all blows over.'

'It won't blow over,' Malik said.

He made himself a mug of tea, using my hot water. He may be trying to cut down on sugar but he still likes his tea with large amounts of milk. At his home, his wife, Mona, makes tea with boiled milk. It makes me want to vomit just thinking about it. But that is the way of the world: one man's meat is another man's poison. Unless you are in the Middle East, where one man's Mede is another man's Persian.

'You mean, they won't go away.'

'People like Zoltan Khan. I know these people. They will not stop till they have their revenge.'

'And that revenge will entail -'

113

'Cutting you, Mr Rubin -'

'Are we talking about certain soft tissues here, Malik?' I said, and smiled.

'It is nothing to smile about, Mr Rubin They will try to kill you. They will never stop. You insulted Zoltan's wife. You destroyed her car. You took that girl -'

'Anna.'

'You took her off the streets. She is their property.'

'Oh no, she isn't,' I said.

Malik sipped his tea. Found it too hot.

'You say that you do not believe. Not in God. Allah. Not in right and wrong. But you still want to help this girl. This I do not understand.'

'Me neither,' I said.

'So why do you do these things? We waste time and need to make money for the business. You tell me it is about making profit. No profit, no business.'

'That's true,' I said.

I looked out over the Square again. At the Station Hotel. At the railway station, with its grand façade. The neo-classical style, the station is well known in architectural circles for its classical portico of the Corinthian order, consisting of six columns in width and two in depth, which dominates the Square, where it is located. It has lasted since 1846 so it cannot be long before the philistines who run our council decide to demolish it, and erect a mosque in its place.

I turned to look at Malik. His face betrayed his worry and his sadness. He has no wish to die young, leaving Mona a widow and his children orphans. For myself, I have not wife, no children, and my one relative, my mother, no longer recognises me. Visiting her seems a waste of time, energy and petrol, but I still visit, from time to time. Yet, for all my lack of ties, I too have no wish to die, ore even be cut East Europeans working for scum like Zoltan Khan.

So why do I put myself in danger? I do not know the answer, any more than Malik does. It is not even out of a desire to cleanse the country, or this city, of scum and crime. That is impossible, especially when the powers-that-be themselves refuse, for several base motives, to make moves against Pakistani criminals. And in the process hobble the police who would like to do something.

Nor even, for that matter, from a wish to assist young kids like Anna. For all I knew, drugged up to her eyeballs, she was sometimes an occupant of a Nirvana I would never experience or understand.

'What are you planning for tomorrow, Malik?'

He shrugged his shoulders.

'Is it up to me?'

'What do you mean by that?' I said.

Again he shrugged. "Seems like I sit here and wait for Zoltan to kill me.'

'No,' I said, ' I am the one he wants. Trust me on that. But I have suggested you go away. Bugger off to Pakistan for a couple of months..'

'Tomorrow, I am going up to the Lake District. To visit my mother. 'You can accompany me, if you wish.'

'Will they let me in?' he asked foolishly.

'You wait outside. Enjoy the scenery. Then afterwards we drive round to Coniston. Coniston Water. John Ruskin. Beautiful scenery there.'

My mother would not recognise me, would be unable to talk about my father, our life in South Africa, after my father had rescued her from Soviet-occupied Lithuania. She does not know whether she is on a tram or in an aeroplane. She is incontinent and sleeps much of the time, which is how the nursing staff like it; while she sleeps, she is not making demands.

Esther Hagar, who married David Rubin, was always a fastidious woman and she would be deeply ashamed if she were aware that she is now doubly incontinent.

'You want to- '

Malik stopped.

'What?'

'No, it's not my business, Mr Rubin'

'Spit it out, Malik.'

'OK! You are going to see your mother. To say.....to say, goodbye.'

I shook my head and smiled grimly. I saw people scurrying

to and from the railway station. I drank the last of my mug of tea.

Malik was right, damn him. Yes, I was going to say farewell to my mother, just in case. Except........except I had no intention of dying, not just yet. Not for a few years yet.

Chapter Fifteen

I parked up by the office, round the corner near the Chinese buffet. No parking meter wardens, this time of the evening.

Kids in various states of intoxication made noise outside boozers and clubs. It was still too early for a rumpus. That would come later, after the ritual baiting of the cops, the vomiting all over the street, and the consumption of yet more alcohol.

New Street is now indistinguishable from any other city centre. American takeaway franchises and numerous charity shops.

At the end of the street, the change begins. It is abrupt. You are smacked in the face by a strong wind blowing down two valleys and coming together her. Chapel Hill is broad and steep. The right hand side is all takeaways: Punjabi, mostly, but in recent years a few Kurdish, Turkish. No Chinese in this section of the town. One fish and chip shop, where they use oil for cooking, and in my opinion fish and chips never taste right unless they are cooked in lard, animal fat. I pay no mind to ancient Mosaic laws.

I was dressed in baggy trousers and a long-sleeved shirt. It would be cooler later on and I'd left a pullover in the car. On my feet, hidden by the length of my trousers, were my boots. They are strong, comfortable, and I always feel good when wearing them.

It was important not to look like a cop or a man on a mission. Let it be casual. I was a punter looking for sex. Play it cool and careful, Jack.

I passed an old yard, something built toward the end of the nineteenth century. Cannot remember the name: Sykes's Yard, something like that. The first thing I saw was the lighted cigarette. I pretended not to see, and continued walking slowly.

Further down, near the river, where an old mill and dye-works had once stood, but was now a gym and sports centre, I stopped. I gazed at the river, and was careful not to look around me, careful not to be seen observing. I turned and walked slowly along past the bright takeaways. There was nothing there to attract me. Chicken in not my favourite food, and certainly not from a rat-infested room where the staff smoke, do not always observe full hygiene. The Kashmiri takeaway seemed no better and whoever was the person who had devised the hand-written sign acclaiming Balti curries has not been successful at school in English classes. If I had ever written *baLti currie's*, I'd have been cuffed round the ears by the teacher. I stopped to look at the window.

The guy from the yard was walking slowly toward me.

He was a white man but even as the dusk enveloped the evening I could tell from his facial features that he was from Eastern Europe. Something about the Slav cheekbones.

'You lookin' for somethin' good, mate?'

119

'Well, I was wondering....'

'Yeah?'

He was a short guy and he had a barrel chest. His arms were probably strong.

'Where does a guy get .....y'know.......'

'You wanting sex?' he said.

Except the word came out as *sheshk*.

I nodded.

'Can you help me?'

I was playing the part of the shy punter, hungry for it, but frightened to ask.

'What you lookin' for?' he asked, and he lit another cigarette.

'Not mutton,' I said. 'Lamb. Young and fresh.'

He flashed me a smile. I caught a glimpse of gold-capped teeth.

'You come wid me,' he said.

I followed him into Sykes's Yard. I was ready for him. If he tried to relieve me of my wallet, I'd smack those prominent cheek bones faster than you could say Peter Tchaikovsky.

Further into the yard, and I saw old houses. I could hear the sound of water, and realised it was water, a bend in the river.

'Forty,' the man said and held out his hand.

'Sorry?'

'You want young, forty bucks.'

'Ah, yes, now I understand.' I paused. 'How much for....very young?'

He looked round, ensuring no one could hear him. He leaned in closer. I could smell the rankness of his sweat and cigarette smoke. Don't let anyone persuade you that prostitution is an exciting exchange of pleasure. First comes the haggling over cash. And that is cash in hand – no cheques, mate no debit cards.

'I got nice school kid. Beautiful girl.'

'How old?'

He almost whispered the answer. 'Only twelve years.'

I found a gulp from, somewhere in my throat.

'Twelve years old.'

'You want?'

"Also forty pounds?' I said.

He stifled laughter.

'This young meat. I give for eighty bucks.'

'Eighty?'

'OK! I give for seventy. Short time.'

'Short time?' I said, ever the ignorant punter, possibly a first timer at this game.

'Twelve years. Fifteen minutes. Seventy bucks. Good offer.'

'Where is this girl?' I said.

121

He took hold of my arm, roughly, anxious to get my seventy quid, and then back outside to entice another sucker.

He led me to one of the old houses, one of four that had formed a square. He inserted a key into a door. Opened the door.

There was a flight of narrow stairs. Quite steep, too. No handrail. These had been dwellings for workers, possibly hands at the mill and dye-works in other times. In these sunless houses were wives knocking out kids on an annual basis. Rickets prevalent, because of the lack of sunshine. No bath, no inside toilet. Slavery takes many forms.

The man pointed to the flight of steps.

'No,' I said,' you go up first.'

He pointed again. No way was he going to take the lead. No way was he going to be taken from behind. This guy might have a poor command of the English language but he was no fool.

I climbed the steps, taking trouble not to seem too agile, nor too keen.

At the top of the stairs, on narrow landing, there were two doors. The man ignored the first door. He unlocked a second door.

An electric connection swung dangerously from the ceiling. There was a single bulb. Enough to give light. Not good enough for reading. But people did not enter this room in order to read or otherwise feed the mind. This was a place for that most basic of transactions, *sex.*

A girl sat on the edge of the bed. She barely looked up when

I entered. But I could tell immediately that she was probably older than twelve years, but it could have been that the life she was leading, whether willingly or unwillingly – and I'd place bets on it being the latter – had aged her prematurely.

I could also see that this girl was not Anna.

'You like?' the man asked.

I led him out of the room.

'I give you one hundred for very, very young,' said.

He lit a cigarette from the butt of the one he had almost finished. He ground the butt under the sole of dirty trainer shoes.

'One hundred pounds,' I said softly. 'For very fresh meat.'

He locked the bedroom door. Seemed to be deciding on something. I did not need to be a clairvoyant to know what was troubling the bastard. In the other room he had young meat but she was not for sale right now. But this was the attraction of one hundred big ones. That kind of offer is hard to resist, especially if it were possible to put it on one side, and not give a percentage to Zoltan Khan.

His mind was resolved. He unlocked the other door. Only a fraction, mind you. He allowed me to peer inside.

'You like?' he said hoarsely.

Like the other room this too was small, and lit by a single bulb. There was a dirty bed on which rested a thin eiderdown.

I felt a lump rise in my my throat.

There, on the floor, between the bed and a radiator, was

huddled the girl. Her short hair was dirty and dishevelled, her face smeared with dust and blood. The way she was huddled, it was clear that she was cuffed at the wrists.

I pretended to pant loudly. Or maybe I was not pretending, for I felt anger rising inside of me.

'You want?' the man asked.

'I want,' I said.

He quickly pulled me back out of the room and closed the door.

'One hundred bucks, you give.'

I reached into my back pocket. Took out five times twenty notes. Handed them over to the man, whose ugly face I wanted to reduce to bloodied pulp.

He placed my money in the wad he was happy to let me see. Malik does the same. It is their way of reminding people how well they are doing.

'You wait. I clean girl's face.'

'No, no,' I said urgently. 'She's OK as she is.'

He shrugged his shoulders. In this business, as he had learned long ago, there is no accounting for individual taste.

He checked his watch.

'One hundred bucks, so I give you twenny minutes, OK?'

I did a bit of dumb show, bringing my wrists together.

He looked dubious at first but soon brightened. He gave me the key to unlock the handcuffs.

I went inside the room.

I removed my shirt and hung it over the keyhole. I looked at the ceiling and the corners for evidence of a camera but could see nothing. But that did not mean we were not being observed. Some men will pay to watch others.

I knelt down beside Anna. So far, she had not screamed. She had noted who I was. She actually seemed pleased to see me. Her smile was thin but it was there, on her face. I unfastened the cuffs. She started to rub her skin. Not the wisest thing to do, but this was no time to be giving her instruction.

I checked the curtained window. There were thick burglar bars right across. It would need Arnold Schwarzenegger in Terminator mode to break those bands of steel.

I lifted Anna on to the bed. She did not resist. She seemed as light as a feather. I guessed they had not been plying her with much food since they had taken her from Malik's place.

'Mr Rubin......'

I placed my hand over her mouth. Shook my head, signing her to remain silent.

If we were being observed, then the watcher was not getting any titillation for his money.

If, on the other hand, we were being watched by the Slav, then on his return I could not expect a Thank you and being wished on my way.

I did exercises with my hands, flexing my fingers, and told Anna to do the same. She needed to be able to move quickly.

Then I made her stand up and do exercises. I wanted to get the blood throwing through the arteries and veins of that sad slim body. Once we were out of there, we would both have to be able to move fast.

I was pleased with myself. Silcock had been right. He clearly had intelligence on which he had not been allowed to act. Sure, he was using me, but I was not going to be the one to complain.

The guy had promised me twenty minutes with his dirty little Lolita. He was a crook. He knocked on the door after only fourteen minutes.

I signalled for Anna to move away from the door, to sit on the bed.

I stood to the left of the door. The handle turned. The Slav came in. I hit him hard on the side of the head, in the temporal region. That usually knocks them down for some considerable time. Not this guy: the bastard must have been made from concrete. Next thing I saw, he had a blade in his hand.

This was no time for the rules laid down by the Marquess of Queensbury, Oscar Wilde's nemesis. There never is such a time.

The guy was young and strong. So am I. One major difference between us: he was a heavy smoker, and could not last the distance. We wrestled, we thrashed about on the floor and the bed. The noise must have carried. At last, though, I was able to bang his thick skull against the burglar bars. He sank to the ground, bloody and heaving for breath.

I stepped back, to avoid any trap. But he was sinking fast.

Just to help him sink further and more deeply, I kicked him hard on the side of his head. These boots are made for more than walking.

I put on my shirt. That would hide most of the blood and bruises. I took hold of Anna's hand. To my surprise, she reached up and kissed me on my cheek.

'Stop that, you little tart,' I said harshly. 'We're not out of the woods yet.'

I was tired and hurt, but remembered to take back my one hundred quid from his wad.

We walked fast up Chapel Hill and crossed the ring road where the planners put traffic first and the hapless pedestrian second.

We crossed at last. I looked back. We were being pursue by three guys with long black coats and vengeful looks.

I dragged Anna up to the bus station. In spite of the late hour, there were still plenty of people about. Town centres are now like that: places to booze, eat inedible shit from polystyrene plates or even buckets, and to vomit.

Once again, old movies came to my aid. This time an old Cary Grant thriller made with Hitchcock. (Hitchcock wanted to be Gary Grant. And so did Archie Leech himself.)

I approached two female CSO. Community Support Officers. Blunkett bobbies.

'Can you say where the Bus Station is?'

Neither spoke. One used a thumb to indicate a large sign

close by.

'I'll bet that thumb s seen some service,' I said.

'What's that sup;posed to mean?' the fatter of the two asked.

'Well, you are lesbians, aren't you?'

A small crowd had gathered. Among them, mean, anxious to beat shit out ODF me and take back Anna, were the three guys with high cheek bones.

'Go home, mate, cr we arrest you,' the second woman said.

'You don't have powers of arrest, Herman,' I said.

She was on her mobile phone. Thank God for that.

'Who's the girl?'

'She's mine,' I said. 'Paid good money for the whole night.'

Both of them had eyes wide open. I must be a nut case.

'Gave fifty quid to the woman who runs the care home. Good money, I thought.'

One had her cuffs ready. She moved toward me.

There was a murmur of disapproval from the bystanders. No sympathy for the law from those chav tossers.

Three police cars arrived. The cavalry. Considering the central police station is only a few yards down the road, they'd taken an unconscionable time arriving. Would have been quicker to walk.

Tasers and batons were to hand. Two female

officers took hold of Anna. I was thrown to the ground.

Cuffed and slammed and slapped around. I adopted the foetal position, the better to protect my cods. Batons fell. I ceased to feel pain after the first four or five blows.

'Stand him up,' a voice said.

I was dragged to my feet.

'Well, if it isn't our David, Mrs Lunn's little boy boy.'

Lunn advanced on my with his baton, struck me in the middle of my back. I went down. Felt no pain. In fact, I was smiling.

The Hitchcock movie? *North by North West*. Remember how Roger Thornhill, impeccably played by Cary Grant, is in a saleroom and deliberately gets himself arrested in order to escape foreign agents? All those hours watching movies. I knew it would come in useful one day.

I had no chance to check on my three guys. They had probably melted away as soon as the cop cars arrived on the scene.

Chapter Seventeen

'You'd have made a bloody good copper, Jack,' Silcock said.

We were sitting outside a public house, enjoying the warm sunshine, and the gentle sound of the stream running by.

Silcock was well on the way. Because he was not driving, he was ale to pour beer after beer down his throat. I, on the other hand, was driving but would not have taken much alcohol even if I'd been a passenger. I like to keep my wits about me.

From time to time, Silcock calls me on my cell phone, invites me to join him for a jar. Always the same place – well away from town, away form prying eyes. I could see the local newspaper article. Chief Superintendent sups with dubious private detective. All kinds of innuendos as to why such a friendship was detrimental to good policing. Was Mr Silcock protecting this man, whose background was in South Africa, and whose father had been murdered. A man who was aged thirty-five years and who had not yet been married.

So why did Silcock choose my company, from time to time? It was not as friendship. There was no suggestion of a working relationship. No money was coming my way from the county force. I think he liked the way I told it as it was. No namby-pamby words. No slimy political correctness.

'I'd have made a lousy cop, Mr Silcock. I wouldn't have fit in.'

'I'm amazed you got in I the first place. Most Jews who apply just happen to have flat feet.'

'How many times do I have to tell you? I am not a Jew. I'm an atheist.'

Silcock emptied his pint glass.

'Anna got away safely,' he said.

'Back to Lithuania?'

'Her mother came to collect her. Tears all over the office. Real tears. Genuine.'

I'd not been allowed to see Anna. Red tape. I was not a relative. Not even as close friend. One thing I did learn: she was well and truly free of drugs. Once the Slavs had taken possession of her again, after they had snatched her from Malik's place, they had punished her by withholding all drugs. This was the best punishment she could have received. Now she was clean.

'So what happens next?' I said.

Silcock exploded. 'Don't you want to know more about Anna?'

I shook my head.

'No.'

'You're a heartless bastard, Mr Rubin.'

'She was nothing to me.'

131

'You almost lost your life,' Silcock said softly. 'You care about that, don't you?'

'Sure. That's what life's about. Survival. Nothing else.'

'No aim? No purpose?'

I took a sip of my lager shandy.

'Men wiser and more learned than I have discerned in history a plot, a rhythm, a predetermined pattern. These harmonies are concealed from me.'

'Another of your clever quotes, Jack?' Silcock said tolerantly.

'H A L Fisher. A History of Europe,' I said. 'You should try it, Silcock. Beats reading the Sun.'

Ducks swam in the stream. People threw bread and cakes to them. What did ducks do before stupid people encouraged their children to feed the ducks? They didn't starve.

'We were able to close down a couple of takeaways in Chapel Hill,' Silcock said. Including the Kashmir. On Health and Safety grounds. No mention of prostitution. Young kids, that kind of thing. Ciggie butts on the kitchen floor and poor hygiene facilities for the staff.'

'And that little bastard, Viktor?'

'I applied for him to be deported. An order was made.'

'But....'

'Yep! He appealed and some liberal judge allowed him to remain in this country indefinitely. On the grounds he had put down roots here.'

'Where is he now?' I said.

'Not in this town,' Silcock said. 'He'd better not set his foot here again.'

'So.........that only leaves Zoltan Khan.'

'Sorry, Jack. But he's untouchable.'

'For you, maybe. But for me....'

'Let it go, Jack,' Silcock said earnestly. 'If he doesn't trouble you or Malik....it aint worth it, my son.'

We stood up. Walked to the the car, parked out at the back. I unlocked the driver's door.

'No central locking, Jack?' Silcock said.

'Can't afford it,' I said. 'I don't earn one hundred and sixty k a year.'

'More like two hundred thou,' he said, laughing. 'What with bonuses and benefits.'

'It could have been yours as well, you know.'

He belched.

'Silcock, don't vomit in my car.'

He had gone a green colour.

I reached over and opened the door at his side.

Just in time, too. He leaned out and was sick. A real Technicolor rainbow.

I kept a bottle of water in the car. Gave it to Silcock to clean out his mouth.

He recovered quickly.

On the drive back, we were mostly silent. What had needed to be said, had been said.

Then, out of nothing, Silcock said: 'That wife of Zoltan's.....'

'Kavita.'

'Quite a looker, they tell me.'

'I wanted to shag her,' I said.

'No chance now.'

'Never say never,' I said.

'That dick of yours will get you into trouble, Jack,' Silcock said.

'It already has,' I said. 'Many times.'

Again a silence, but I could tell that Silcock was not yet finished.

'Get it off your chest, Silcock,' I said.

'Get what?'

'Whatever it is that's on your mind.'

'I'll tell you truthfully,' Silcock said. 'Zoltan is still peddling young flesh. And I don't like it. I want him off my patch, but -'

'You don't know how to achieve it,' I said.

'I need your help, Jack. You are the one man in this city -'

'Get lost, Silcock,'I said. 'Whatever I decide, it's for me, Jackis Rubin. Not for you. Not for the county force. Not for Anna, either.' I paused, and then said, forcefully, 'It'll be for me, Silcock, me alone.'

Chapter Eighteen

Arthur was different and the world has ignored him. Among 19th century philosophers, Arthur Schopenhauer was the first to contend that, at its core, the universe is not a rational place. Since his death in 1860, his philosophy has had a special attraction for those who wonder about life's meaning.

I've stopped wondering about life's meaning. Gave up when I was an adolescent. My mother, overcome by severe dementia, stuck there in her Lakeland prison, never read Schopenhauer or any other philosopher, and wouldn't have been any better if she had. Suffering is permanent, obscure and dark, And shares the nature of infinity.

That was said by another denizen of the Lake District. He had a large beak too. I wonder, in my mad way: was Wordsworth a Jew?

There was absolutely no reason why I should want to destroy Zoltan Khan. By putting him out of business, out of circulation, I was changing nothing, achieving nothing, except for a stupid minor and very local victory.

Yet I wanted to finish him off. I wanted to burn down his large and pretentious house. I wanted to see him in jug. I wanted him dead, the bastard. And the only reason for my loathing was the fact that I fancied shagging his proud wife. Once would be enough, and after that all the turmoil swilling round in my brain would be gone. Until next time, at least.

'Malik, hold the fort. I'm going to walk on to the library.'

My colleague could see I was in what he called one of my moods. He nodded his assent.

I arrived at the library. It is, in fact, a library and art gallery. I went in to the lending library. So many books and I was not sure what I was looking for. I've long since given up hope of finding a book that will explain to me what life is all about and why we are on this spinning planet.

I walked across the the literature shelves. American and British literature. And there she was, running a finger delicately along the line of books.

'Hi!'

No way did I want to come on strong.

'Hi,' she said, and she smiled.

'Looking for anything particular?' I said.

'The Rubaiyat of Omar Khayyam,' Kavita said.

'Follow me,' I said gently.

She followed me. I was doing better than expected.

I led the way to the poetry section. There were several

translations of the poem. I chose one with Edward Fitzgerald's picture on the front.

'Here you are, Madam.'

'Kavita,' she said, and laughed, showing good white teeth.

'Kavita,' I repeated.

'It means poetry.' she said. 'It's my Hindu name.'

'But I thought -'

'Yes, I am Muslim. I think my father thought it was a pretty name.'

'He was right,' I said. 'A pretty name for a beautiful woman.'

'Anyway, thanks for your help, Mr -'

'Jack Rubin.'

She was making her way to the exit. I had to move fast.

'Call me Jack,' I said.

Now we were outside, looking down on the concrete awfulness of the Piazza.

'Fancy a coffee?' I said.

She shrugged her shoulders.

'Why not? She said. 'But nothing too public.'

'I know just the place, Kavita.'

We did not walk together. She followed me at a discreet distance. We walked along Shambles and on to Cross Church Street. Opposite us was the Parish Church. In the crypt there is a café. No chance of being seen there. Not by Zoltan Khan, anyway.

We ordered two cups of coffee and biscuits and sat at a table in a corner.

Kavita was wearing her traditional sari gear with soft trousers. I wondered what was underneath.

'So you like poetry,' I said.

'Is this a cathedral?' Kavita said.

'No, but it is a Christian church.'

'You are a Christian?'

I shook my head. "I'm an atheist. And I don't think anyone is going to look for an atheist and a Muslim in a Christian church.

She looked at me closely. I thought it was a long stare of endearment. But then, being besotted, I would, wouldn't?

'Jack-'

'Yes?'

'Why did you burn my beautiful Impreza?'

Mr Rubin, I know it's none of my business,' Malik said.

I knew what he was going to say.

'Then keep your mouth shut,' I said.

'You're making as fool of yourself,' he said.

I knew he was right but I could not help myself. I was in the grip of a fever.

'I don't want to talk about it,' I said.

'Well, I do!' Malik said, with unaccustomed vehemence. 'The business – you've done nothing for three weeks. The funds are low.'

Since our meeting in the library, Kavita and I had been seeing other almost every day over three weeks. We met in the crypt café; up in the hills, where we walked on paths skirted by bilberries and heather; and twice in the local cinema, for matinees. Malik was right, of course: I was neglecting the business.

'I'll soon build up the bank account again,' I said. 'Trust me, Mr Malik.'

He shook his head dolefully.

'You won't be able to build up your body again.'

'What?'

'After Zoltan has finished with you,' Malik added.

Do you think I'm afraid of Zoltan Khan?' I said, flaring up.

'You're not afraid of anybody or anything. That's your problem,' Malik said.

He put water in the kettle and switched on.

'Tea?'

'No, thanks, Malik.' And then I said, 'I'm going out this afternoon.'

'Kavita?'

'Yes.'

Malik brewed tea for himself. We have a rule in the office, that each man makes his own tea. We have a second rule, too – no discussion of religion.

'You always fancy Asians, don't you?' Malik said.

'Only Asian women,' I said. 'You are safe, Mr Malik.'

'He shook his head. He could see I was moving to a place where he could not help me. I was aware that I had already moved to a place where I could not help myself. The fever that gripped me could only be lifted by getting Kavita laid. I felt certain the day was not far off.

'You've never gone on like this before,' I said. 'And there have been others.'

"Yes, but the other weren't married to Zoltan Khan.'

'So?'

'So,' Malik said, 'the others would not want to kill you. Only cut off your testicles.'

'I like the delicacy of your language, Mr Malik,' I said, laughing. 'I have never heard you swear or cuss or make an oath.'

'Did you say you were going to the cinema this afternoon?' And paused. 'The multiplex?'

"No, we're going out of town. There's a little picture house that shows classic movies. It's a matinee. Kavita can't get out in the evening.'

'That must be heart-breaking for you both,' Malik said, trying a bit of unaccustomed irony.

'I'm taking her to see *Casablanca*.'

'A waste of time,' Malik said.

'I don't agree. You'd be surprised how much you can learn from the movies.

Chapter Nineteen

The movie started at two. I waited. Kavita did not turn up.

I kept checking the time on my cell phone. The days when I wore a wrist watch are long gone, for me and for many others. No way was I going inside on my own. I have seen this movie many times. Yes, it's a classic. It isn't *The Maltese Falcon* and it has many plot and other weaknesses, but the film overall is a beauty.

After thirty minutes I concluded that Kavita wasn't going to come. I assumed there must be a problem at home. However, to make assurance doubly sure, I went to check the car park. Her car wasn't there. She was very happy with that car, I knew; there had been no problems getting a speedy pay-out from the insurance company.

I returned to the front of the cinema. Black rain clouds were gathering in the sky. We have had a wet summer this year. We have a wet summer every year. And still no sign of the beautiful woman. So it was back to the car park and my Volvo, that badly needed a wash and wax. I decided to go home and take a shower. But not a wax; I am not yet victim to that kind of narcissism.

As I opened the door,m with my key – nothing fancy or

modern such as central locking on my old banger – a car was driven fast into the car park. I turned with a smile on my face. Kavita had been able to make it after all. Two men jumped out of the car, one while it was still moving. There were white guys, but, as I could tell immediately, from Eastern Europe. One guy had a knife. No problem. I could deal with him. But the second man held a gun in his hand and I'm no Superman, able to catch bullets in his teeth.

They rough-housed me. There was no need. Faced with that hand gun I'd have got in the back seat of their wreck without argument or trouble. I was with the armed man, while the knife man slipped quickly into the driver's seat.

All the way on the drive back to the city, no word was spoken. Mebbe these two guys knew no English. Maybe they were poor conversationalists in any language. I got to thinking where we might be going. I did not think it would be Lakenwood. Nevertheless, I felt sure they were working for Zoltan Khan.

I was surprised to note that we were going up toward the moors, and actually passed by on the road next to my place. I stole a glance but there was no activity. Zoltan was not about to burn my place down.

We reached the high plateau. For several weeks there has been heavy rain – heavy for these summer months, that is - and the peat and bracken were very wet. No way this moorland would burn this year. I'd the feeling, however, that I was ripe for burning.

No longer was I thinking of Kavita and how to get between

her thighs. Malik I had forgotten. My mind was focussed now. These guys were taking me somewhere lonely and they were going to kill me. There had to be a way to get away from them.

They stopped the car. My back-seat companion waved his gun. I got out of the car. Who needs language?

Again the guy waved his gun. Unlike what you see in Western movies, hand guns are not exactly accurate, especially if fired in haste and from far off. I had to put distance between him and me.

The reservoirs that provide water a large conurbation are fed by streams from these hills. These streams were now torrents. In order to facilitate the downward movement of water, and decrease los, the water board people had constructed concrete watercourses.

The rain was pouring down now. The man with the gun urged me to go higher. I looked round at the vast openness and could see no other human being. These two guys wanted me to die in a place where my body was unlikely to be discovered, certainly for a considerable period of time. I was going to die out here like a stricken animal. And for what? Lust for a woman. Malik was right. I was foolish. I prefer to say I am a pillock.

I have been told that people about to die lose control of their bowels and bladder. I can believe it. I had to fight to keep control. Inside me a deep resentment well up. Then, just as quickly, my mind became completely clear. I knew what had to do.

We reached a part of the hillside that was green and slippery. Moss clung wetly to smooth stones. I chose to walk

145

across the stones. I held out my arms in order to maintain my balance, and in the hope the two crooks would do the same.

The man with the gun did not have the right balance. He slipped on the wet stones. His partner, close behind, also faltered.

I did not wait to see more. I scrambled quickly upward. I had to put ground between me and the gunman. My legs and lungs found a new power. I tried to run crab-wise, sideways and upwards. I was glad of the rain pouring down.

There was a crack, somewhere near my head. I did not wait to see where the bullet hit the ground. What I knew was, that shot was too close for comfort.

I ran toward the nearest concrete water chute. I hurled myself against the structure, as a second bullet smashed into the concrete and ricocheted away. No way could I wait for a third shot.

I threw myself bodily over the edge of the chute and into the water. The concrete was hard on my body and my head but I was being carried down and away from the killers.

Where the chute ended, there were steps. Eight or nine of them, intended to oxygenate the water before it entered the reservoir. I hit all the steps, one by painful one. And then, biggest shock of all, I hit the ice-cold water. I started to swim. It was a long and painful swim. To tell the truth, I am barely a competent swimmer. Half way across I thought that I could go no further. My leg muscles raged and my rib cage was ready to cave in. But I was not yet ready to die. Will-power alone got me across to the other side. I heaved myself out. I fell exhausted on to the sedge. The rain did nothing to dampen my exhilaration. I had made it. I was still alive, and far away from the would-be killers, who would have the task of telling their boss that they had failed to kill me. I burst out laughing.

I struck out across the plateau and came at last to the winding moorland road. This road was once a busy route, until the motorway was constructed, so that now it has almost reverted to what is used to be, a pack horse road.

The first vehicle that came along was a sports car, driven by a young man wearing a scarf, and with a blonde by his side. I waved to them to stop. Cheeky sods, they waved back cheerfully, but did not stop. The next car was a saloon car with an old couple inside. They looked hard at me but they did not stop either. The third car did stop. It was a police car. Without bothering to ask what had happened, a constable pushed me into the back of the car and took his place beside me. At least, he wasn't pointing a gun at my gut.

'If you could drop me off further down,' I said, 'I have my house there.'

They both laughed.

'It's down to the station with you, lad. And a warm bath.'

Were the two twats blind, or what? Could they not see the bruises on my body, not least on my arms?

'Stop at my house,' I said, in a voice that I hoped was authoritative. 'I need a drink.'

'Sure you do,' the copper said. 'We'll stop and get you whisky and soda.'

'If you drive past my house, I'll make sure you are shit on from a great height by Chief Superintendent Silcock.'

The driver slowed down considerably.

'And then I shall be talking to the Chief Constable, Sir Radley James Dickerson.'

'Do you....you know the CC, do you?' the driver said.

'We meet monthly, at the Rotary Club.'

That was all I needed. I was soon in my house and enjoying a warm shower. This helped to ease the pain in my body.

Afterwards, in dressing gown and slippers, looking out at the rain still falling, I telephoned Malik. I had a Volvo to collect.

Chapter Twenty

Behind the washing machine – a Hotpoint, if you must know – I keep a small locked box. This is a good hiding place. I doubt that few thieves ever check behind washing machines.

Inside the box, also locked, is a smaller box. It pays to be careful, especially when the item one is hiding is a hand gun. Unregistered and unlicensed.

I heard a car approaching the house and stop. I looked out of the window. It was Malik in his new Merc. Like Kavita he had also benefited from an insurance pay out. Cash for crash. I was not surprised to see him: after all, I had asked him to visit.

Malik came into the house; the door was not locked. I offered him tea but when he discovered I only had herbal tea, and neither milk nor sugar, he declined, and opted for a glass of water instead. My water tastes good. It comes from a deep spring, and is always cold and free from chemicals.

I started to strip down the Browning.

'Now I am sure you are mad,' Malik said, a worried look on his face that furrowed his brow.

'I've never been more sane,' I said.

I held the gun in my hand.

'This is a Browning hand gun,' I said. 'The last hand gun that Browning made. 9 mm, and he patented it.'

'Murder is murder, Mr Rubin.'

'This isn't for murder. This is for self-defence.'

'And all for a tart,' Malik said.

'If I didn't know different, I'd say you didn't like women,' I said.

'They brought evil into the world. Shatan made Eve eat of the -'

'Don't you dare start that religious shit,' I said vehemently. 'And certainly not in this house.'

He spread his hands despairingly.

'And it isn't about Kavita. It's about Anna and those other kids who are groomed by bastards who deserve to be shot.'

'You haven't been thinking straight since you first saw her,' Malik said.

'I'm over that,' I said.

His eyes lit up. 'Finished?'

'The fever has lifted. I am well again.'

'I know what you mean,' Malik said. 'While the fever is....'

'Raging?'

'Yes. You can't think straight. All you want to do is talk about her, mention her name over and over again. And you're unable to take advice.'

'Your diagnosis is correct, Dr Malik,' I said. 'And you sound as if you've been there yourself.'

'There was this girl I met. She lived in Widnes. My father warned me. My mother cried. But we still eloped together.'

'But you didn't marry her, did you?'

'We went on a trip round Europe. We stayed in good hotels. We ate in good restaurants. We walked on the beach in the evening, hand in hand.'

'And then your money ran out,' I said.

'How did you know?' Malik asked.

'I guessed.'

In fact, he had mentioned this girl many times before, and I suspected he still carried a torch for her. As we all do for a first love.

I can strip the Browning down to its six essential parts in a matter of minutes, and I'm no expert. It is accurate and takes most standard ammo. The magazine takes thirteen shots and there's another in the breach. That ought to prove enough for my purposes.

'If anything happens to me, and I don't expect it will, make sure the payments for my mother are made monthly.'

Malik nodded seriously.

'This is something you have to do, isn't it, Mr Rubin?' he said.

'Yes, and I don't know why.'

Malik shook my hand solemnly.

'See you tomorrow morning,' I said.

I drove slowly down to Lakenwood. Plenty of time. I'd arranged with Zoltan to be at his place by eight o'clock. It was still light and there was no rain.

There were no guards on his house – none I could see, that is.

Kavita's Subaru was there. It didn't matter whether or not I saw her; my fever was at an end.

I rang the bell. Zoltan Khan answered the door himself.

'As-Salāmu Alaykum.'

I did not answer.

He took me through to a room at the back. He gestured for me to sit in a deep easy chair. I shook my head, and sat on an upright chair, next to a table.

He did not offer me food or drink and if he had I'd have told him to shove it up his brown hairy arse.

'You wanted to meet me, Mr Rubin.'

'Your hired two goons to try and kill me,' I said.

'You tried to steal my wife,' Zoltan replied.

'And where is the lovely Kavita?'

'I have sent her back to Pakistan.'

'Not cut into small pieces and spread over the Derbyshire

Moors?' I said.

'In Pakistan, with her family.'

I took the Browning pistol out of my pocket, and laid it down on the table top.

Zoltan smiled. He stood up, went to a roll-top desk, and took out his own gun, and placed it on the desk beside him.

I smiled in return. He was sitting in a deep easy chair. I looked across at his pistol. The safety catch was off. Mine too.

'Two men with a gun,' I said. 'And I tell you now, I will not fire first.'

'Nor I,' Zoltan Khan said.

'I think you will be the first to go for your gun,' I said, never taking my eyes from him.

'You are a fool, Mr Rubin,' he said.

'Everyone tells me so. They also tell me that you are a lecher, a trader in human flesh. Young girls for prostitution. They tell me you work with gangsters from Russia and other places in Eastern Europe.'

'With this, my friend, you expect me to go for my gun the first?' Zoltan said, and he smiled his devious smile.

'I am not your friend, Khan.'

'They tell me that you are a Jew bastard, and I believe that Hitler's Final Solution was the right one.'

I breathed deeply, in order to remain calm and alert.

'I am not a Jew,' I said. 'I detest all religion.'

'Then you cannot expect,' he said, still with that smile on his lips, mirthless and cruel, 'to go to heaven.'

Seventy two virgins and all that shit,' I said.

Still his hand did not move.

'This I believe,' Zoltan said.

'Well, you would, wouldn't you? You being a rotten pander who supplies little children for prostitution.' And I added: 'And when I call you a pancer, Zoltan, I'm not referring to cuddly black and white bears that eat grass and bamboo shoots.'

I could tell from his eyes that I had lost him.

'Then what are you talking about?' he said savagely.

'I'm talking about Pakistan. A failed state. A country that never should have been.'

'What do you mean, Mr Rubin?'

'Jinnah could not be leader of a united India so he invented Pakistan.'

'This is not what my history books tells me,' Zoltan said. 'Are you saying that Pakistan is not a good country?

'What I am saying to you, Zoltan, is this. That your Jinnah, your beloved leader, your so-called Quaid-e-Azam, your great leader, liked white women and lots and lots of whisky.'

Zoltan's calm was beginning to evaporate. I could see a tremor developing in both hands.

'That is enough, Rubin,' Zoltan barked roughly.

'No, not enough. I am saying that if Jinnah were alive now,

he'd be a pander too. Supplying little girls across border.'

Zoltan made his move. As I knew he would.

I had the Browning in my hand. I felt the air move as his bullet went past my head. I fired at his legs, and hit him in the right knee.

Now I was on my feet. The gun had spun from Zoltan's hand.

'You should see more movies, Zoltan,' I said.

He was sobbing with pain and clutching his shattered knee joint.

'Try watching the end of *Shane*. See how Shane makes Wilson draw first.'

I kicked his gun out of his reach, walked to the door.

I turned.

'Oh, and if it's any consolation to you, Khan.....

I have a lot of time for Jinnah, as a man and as a leader.'

'Please help me,' he sobbed.

Pain can make a man squeal. A shattered patella is a lot worse than toothache.

I laughed.

I could hear voices. Family members disturbed by the sound of the bullet and by Zoltan's cries of pain.

'Now leave me alone,' I said. 'You and the bastards who work for you. Or next time I kill you. I mean that, Khan. Next time I kill you.'